THE BARBARY FIGS

RASHID BOUDJEDRA is an Algerian novelist. He has been routinely called one of North Africa's leading writers ever since his debut, *La Répudiation*, was published in 1969, earning the author the first of many fatwas. While he wrote his first six novels in French, Boudjedra switched to Arabic in 1982 and wrote another six novels in the language before returning to French in 1994. His works - including poetry, non-fiction and plays - have been translated into many languages. *The Barbary Figs* (*Les Figuiers de Barbarie*) was awarded the Prix du Roman Arabe 2010.

ANDRÉ NAFFIS-SAHELY is a poet and translator from the French and the Italian. His fables appeared in Island Position's inaugural volume of *Imagine Africa*. His translations include Abdellatif Laâbi's *The Rule of Barbarism* (Island Position) and *The Bottom of the Jar* (Archipelago Books), and Émile Zola's *Money* (Penguin Classics). A selection of his poems is forthcoming in *Oxford Poets 2013*.

THE BARBARY FIGS

RASHID BOUDJEDRA

Translated and with an afterword by André Naffis-Sahely

ARABIA BOOKS

This work is published with support from the French Ministry of Culture.
Ouvrage publié avec le soutien du Centre national du livre.

First published in Great Britain in 2012 by
Arabia Books, 70 Cadogan Place, London SW1X 9AH

Originally published as *Les Figuiers de Barbarie* by Rashid Boudjedra
Copyright © Éditions Grasset & Fasquelle, 2010
English language translation © André Naffis-Sahely, 2012

ISBN 978-1-906697-42-6

Typeset in Garamond by MacGuru Ltd
info@macguru.org.uk

Printed in the US by Edwards Brothers Malloy, Lillington, NC 27546

A CIP catalogue for this book is available from the British Library

Chapter I

THERE HE WAS, dishevelled as always, with that sallow skin and those intense sad eyes! Looking absent-minded in his perennially tieless designer suit. Open-necked shirts in the summer and cashmere pullovers in the winter. This sartorial elegance reminded me of those legendary wardrobes of our youth that contained a dozen luxurious suits, and below which were a dozen pairs of brand-new Italian shoes – their colours matching those of the suits, shirts and pullovers – which emanated a raw, leathery smell that made my head spin, inspiring envy, but above all awe at such extravagance. Those clothes hailed from an alluring elsewhere, a world that we knew only vaguely, with a sense of foreboding and mystery, via its newspapers, books and films.

All the more so since his father's wardrobe, which I'd never seen, was supposedly larger – a vastness that his son's hinted at – and whose range was demonstrated by the father, who wore his suits in a sober, almost soldierly manner. He never wore the same suit, and unlike his son adorned them with the finest ties that often matched the colour of his eyes. Those blue eyes. Or were they topaz? Or turquoise? – it depended on the light and the surroundings. All those suits, which gave him an effeminate, almost timid air; and that mug of his – not a face, but a mug – whose fine features and blonde hair, parted on the left, literally mesmerised everyone he spoke to. That was how strikingly handsome he was, as if his good looks made him highly strung in the company of men, and awkward in the company of women.

Omar, the son, was more ordinary-looking and scrawny, with a swarthy complexion and curly hair. He resembled neither his father nor his mother. He was their antithesis. Their physical opposite, though at heart they were cut of the same cloth. They were very friendly with one another, thick as thieves, but there were no embraces, no tenderness, no nothing. When one saw them together, one quickly understood how fluidly they communicated, as if through a psychic bond.

Omar was almost my age, and as we got older, he pretended to distance himself. As did I. We had nonetheless thought very highly of one another from the first, from the time of those wardrobes full of beautiful suits and gorgeous shoes that he would fling open theatrically each summer when my family and I went to spend our holidays in that small town in the east of Algeria. I was slightly jealous of the treasures that the wardrobe revealed, since I didn't own even a single suit: only two jackets, two pairs of trousers and a single pair of shoes, which I wore until down-at-heel.

This mutual respect, coupled with a sort of admiration, had therefore endured, and on seeing him there, in the departure lounge of Algiers airport – wearing a suit of alpaca fleece of an indeterminate colour, his face consumed by drink and melancholy – I told myself there and then: 'He'll never change!'

When our eyes met, I hurried towards him, despite the fact that he seemed to be taking his time in coming to greet me, although I knew he was itching to. He was merely pretending. It was his way of being coy.

Omar was hungry for tenderness.

I hastened, knowing he was touchy and that despite all his professional success and fine suits, he had become embittered, sad and unhappy.

Our encounters in that airport were not wholly fortuitous. Quite the contrary; they were actual appointments. A ritual we couldn't do without. This had gone on for a very long time. It was all a perverse, confusing and affectionate game.

We kissed, just like that. Politely. Coldly even.

'Hello cousin!' I said, 'Off to Constantine? Of course you are!'

'Hello cousin.' He replied, 'Yes, Constantine. You too, right?'

'How's life?' I asked.

'Bah!' He said, 'As usual, you know. Always on *stand-by*!'

He had studied architecture in the United States for a while and often peppered his sentences with an English word. Without a trace of pretentiousness. Without meaning to. As if inadvertently, or out of shyness.

By the time we had taken our seats on the plane, he said: 'And how's Nana doing? And Mozart? But you know, you never understood any...'

I didn't have time to reply. Or did I say nothing in the end?

We were now sitting comfortably in our seats.

An air hostess said something, but no one took any notice.

Omar had sent me a photo of himself from the bush, a region with a tortured landscape. I had been surprised when the postman handed me the envelope, which contained only a single photograph. I turned it over and looked at the back. There was a place name and a date:

Nothing else. This curtness didn't surprise me in the slightest, and yet the mere fact that he had sent me this photo during that horrifying war overwhelmed me.

It was a photograph of him in military fatigues, slightly blurry, slightly clownish, slightly scratched. I could barely recognise him. It was a photograph that brought to mind other classmates lost to the resistance, to careers, or to foreign cities where they had been exiled: a comical photo, which had taken four months to reach me. Four months to cover 30 miles! It reminded me of those colonial-style, turn-of-the-century photographs, converted into postcards and sold in the dark shops of the big cities. Colonial photographs as bleached and worn as Omar's, which had found its way to me when I least expected it. Bromidic snapshots that set people, buildings and the naked bodies of barely pubescent prostitutes in motion. The photographs were generally comical due to those vulgar colonial expressions that so wretchedly twisted their subjects' faces. I was very young, but already aggravated by those postcards, brimming as they were with such dramatic perverseness that they made me burst out laughing. As if this laughter were a form of catharsis, banishing any thoughts of their indecency, of the expropriation of those nubile bodies, lopsided buildings, or those bearded and moustachioed French soldiers posing in ghastly whorehouses, in those weirdly decorated studios, striking poses so unlikely that they gave the soldiers hilarious, sly expressions.

The photographs were miserable and colonial because they ignored their desired subject's grief, as seen through the eyes of a voracious and cannibalistic other.

This was just as true of the postcards depicting Algerians hanging from worm-eaten gallows, which European Algerians would send to their loved ones, their parents or their friends back in France, emblazoned with the generic caption '*From Algeria with love.*' I had a whole collection of those horrific photographs, which I hid from the rest of my family. Above all from my faint-hearted mother, as well as from Zygote, my younger brother, who was all too capable of sticking them under her nose just to frighten her.

Each time I looked at this photo of Omar, I felt bogged down, caught between hysterical laughter and tears. I could hardly recognise him, apart from the sadness radiating not just from his eyes but from his whole being. Besides, I thought he looked ridiculous in that oversized uniform and crooked cap, with that ancient rifle he hadn't yet learnt to shoulder with pride.

What really upset me, however, was that Omar hadn't scribbled anything more than a place name, Chaabet Lakhra, and a date – 14/05/60 – on the back of that shabby photograph.

Worse still, I was angry that he looked awful in that uniform and that idiotic cap – he whose elegance and wardrobes full of clothes I had found alluring from the very first.

Omar was badly wounded a few weeks after the photo was taken and evacuated to Moscow. He was on this flight, where I so often ran into him, because we both regularly took the shuttle between Algiers and Constantine. I found these all-too-frequent encounters with Omar intriguing. He made the trip for professional reasons, whereas I did it to spend a few weeks in our large family home in Constantine, situated at an altitude of almost 3,000 feet in the dry, invigorating climate I loved so dearly.

Having barely sat down, Omar abruptly said, as if to someone behind me and without looking at me, 'You know, you still haven't understood any of this…' He didn't finish his sentence. I didn't need him to. I knew what he wanted to say because he'd said it time and again since 1962, the year of Independence, when we'd begun our studies at the University of Algiers. We had almost lost touch since we graduated. We merely bumped into each other. It was bizarre. Often by chance. Often because he made sure to appear out of nowhere and block my path so he could tell me about his past, or rather give his own take on his past. Or rather his father's and younger brother's past. Or rather of this sense of guilt… As if we did it on purpose, this bumping into one another. And yet that wasn't the case. Though even if we refused to admit it, we were drawn to one another.

At the beginning, my immediate reaction had been to feel affronted by his attempts to convince me by rattling off the same old speech. Each time we arrived in Constantine, we would while our nights away talking and drinking red wine and whisky. He always began with that irksome, age-old refrain: *You know*… Finally one night, weary of it all, I wound up saying, 'Yes I know, and you're right. Fine, I'm in the wrong. But that's all over and done with. You were exceptional. You didn't shy away from your responsibilities. You followed your own path right through to the end. Swam against the tide. Your time in the bush fighting for the resistance, your brilliance at university, your colossal achievements. You made it. You studied in Chicago! You've become the finest architect in the country. You're known the world over. And to boot,' – I was trying to get a laugh out of him – 'you're the best-dressed man in Algeria. So you know, all the rest, the past… I give up, you're right.'

He flew into a rage. A cold, frightening fury. He was still seething even after emptying a few bottles of wine or a bottle of Scotch: 'So is that what this is all about? You're trying to get one over on me. You say I'm right when you don't actually think so. I don't need your pity... Some more Glenfiddich? No, I don't need your pity because I'm not pathetic. You praise my elegance, my accomplishments, but when it comes to the rest, what really matters to me — because that's the only thing that matters to me – you give in to me as though I were a spoilt child. You let me down...'

I tried to cut him off: 'I don't care about your father and your younger brother. You're my only concern. I loved your father dearly, Omar, but he was a cop! And not just any old cop. Police Commissioner in the toughest, most accursed city during the resistance. The Police Commissioner in Batna throughout the whole war. Batna was hell on earth! Appointed for life. And you – you...'

Omar had fallen silent. I wanted him to fight back, scream, hit me... but he simply retreated into his shell, refilled our glasses and, after an unbearable fifteen minutes of silence, said, 'You never understood...' Then he said nothing more for the rest of the night, just sat there sipping his drink. As if he were dead.

I wound up leaving without even saying goodbye. Without saying a word. He did the same. He sapped my energies. Drove me crazy. I didn't want to play his game, but I always ended up getting mired in his pathological guilt. I began to have my doubts.

That day at the airport in Algiers, as I was boarding the plane to Constantine, I decided to have it out with him, exorcise his demons, relieve him of his grief. I had an hour to persuade him. The duration of the flight between Algiers and Constantine. One hour. Just one hour.

The plane sped down the runaway for take-off.

Chapter II

I'VE NEVER LIKED HAPPY PEOPLE. Happiness has always bored me. Omar was miserable, and that's why I loved him. I relied on his misery and the profound respect I secretly harboured for him. My dealings with him were nonetheless strange. It was not like me to benefit from the misfortunes of others, but I found the drama and confusion surrounding his destiny fascinating, because his experience encapsulated my country's tragic history. It simply radiated out of Omar, his family, his refusal to negotiate the labyrinth of events with honesty and lucidity; a kind of x-ray from which one could read – albeit with difficulty – the collective history of Algeria, one that was both frightening and painful.

I felt saturated with Omar's pain each time I saw him, catching fleeting hints of his mental torture. All those scars my cousin accumulated after those traumatic events were continually exacerbated by fresh additions, each with its own hidden meanings, which could only be distinguished by vague, subtle nuances. These scars were swelled by the effects of a memory that had become confused by dint of his constant brushes with death. Omar had gone from one peril to another, from one loss of consciousness to the next, until his memories had grown heavier and more inward-looking.

Omar had but a single aim in life – to try and escape from the confusion inflicted by that falsified reality, from a father who had collaborated with the French and a brother who worked for the OAS. A reality that had been distorted and disordered for reasons that yet eluded him. He'd been striving to shake off all these gnawing regrets not only since he had first understood his family history, but forever. A genuine symmetry had nonetheless always existed between the various diverging points of view within the family nucleus, which overflowed with emotions, betrayals, acts of cowardice and heroism – both Omar and his grandfather had been staunch nationalists at first and rebels afterwards; with closely related fantasies that were quite capable of suddenly vanishing, contradicting themselves, running up against stubborn fact, disobeying all the known rules of paramnesia, splitting themselves into two, shrinking away, and so on. My relationship with Omar was therefore taxing, but excitingly complex.

He didn't remain in the bush for long. He was gravely wounded after a few months and evacuated to a hospital in Moscow.

Moscow. The hospital. The night scattered into the air where it dissolved. As soon as the first particles of light bombarded the atmosphere, Omar woke up, his limbs numb, debilitated by a psychological weariness whose origins he found difficult to discern. He remembered that the war was over for him and that his leg had been saved. But his first memory was reserved for his favourite filly, Fascination II, as she neighed and galloped at lightning speed, as resplendent as those cast-lead horse statuettes and Omar's grandfather Si Mustafa's beloved Barbary figs that featured on his stable's coat-of-arms and sat on the shelves of Si Mustafa's office alongside the trophies and ribbons he'd won in competitions the world over. Omar never stopped telling himself the war was over. He would then sink into that fluid, silky atmosphere full of his mother Nadia's favourite signs and colours: wine-red, straw-yellow and plum. Nadia was exceptionally beautiful and exuded a bewildering sensuality and energy.

Nadia arranged to go and visit Omar in that distant city... But how had she known that he was in that Moscow hospital? Omar suspected the resistance's efficient but disconcerting intelligence services of helping his mother, who was an informant in the city of Batna, where her husband was Police Commissioner. They had certainly provided her with a fake passport, allowing her to slip past the watchful eye of the French Secret Services in order to arrive, after several detours, in Moscow, the colonial authorities' sworn enemy at the time.

Nadia was laden with gifts and recent photographs of the family and the stud farm's horses, one of which of course was the ever-impressive Fascination II. Omar and I had once witnessed that stunning mare being mounted by a black stallion of exceptional pedigree. I still remember that scene – the violence had both flummoxed and terrified us. The two animals were locked in a savage struggle, egged on loudly by the grooms. Saliva was spraying everywhere. Everyone was excited. That bestial scene had shocked, disgusted and traumatised me.

Nadia came out of nowhere, bringing with her that inimitable mayhem and commotion, wearing an extravagant European-style outfit she had made herself, radiating her cryptic beauty, her sensual exuberance. Omar began asking her for explanations, while that Russian August heat continued to distort objects and the few pieces of furniture in the room, contorting them into curious shapes. All of a sudden, the different layers in the atmosphere grew dense, oscillating between half-darkness and blazing colours, between patches of heavy darkness and shimmering pools of raw light.

The overwhelming atmosphere in the hospital room had become misty and dense, moistening the surface of the mirror with coat after coat of condensation. Determined to show his mother his leg had healed, Omar feebly got out of bed, took a few steps, headed towards the washbasin and combed his hair while looking in the mirror. He gazed at his features, examined them, running his index finger over the skin of his cheeks, which over the past few days had grown rough with stubble. As soon as Omar realised the bristles had grown coarse, the room began to spin. He hung in there, narrowly avoiding falling down or fainting so as not to worry his mother.

Omar then allowed the memories of days past and their distended hours to come flooding back, opening up a horizon of small joys and ordinary sorrows, despite the piling up of uncertainties regarding his mixed Berber, Arab and Turkish origins, and, for the past couple of years – since going into the bush to fight in the resistance – his strange relationship with his father, which had grown complicated in ways he could not have foreseen. Some days he suspected him of collaborating with the colonial authorities, and on others thought him entirely innocent, since he was only following the Organisation's orders advising him to remain in his post as Police Commissioner in Batna to play the part of a double agent. To top it off, ever since his mother had arrived in Moscow, Omar hadn't ceased wondering what role she played in the Organisation.

He often lost himself in a labyrinth of speculation, blood and betrayal, unable to remember who or where he was, despite the presence of his mother, who had a way of sweeping his apprehensions aside with a casual, comical wave of her hand;

whose pathetic movements he observed relentlessly through a kind of bottled-up despair. Like those 19 Sicilian clocks Nadia had brought with her from the city of her birth when she got married, which broke space down into the essential components of time with sumptuous calculation and measured sloth. As if the 19 clocks, which he often thought about but had neither seen nor heard chime, pushed him to the end of his tether and threw him off-kilter, casting him loose in the vast geography of words where he sought refuge in the warm embraces of logic. Yet he remained doubtful. Nadia said: 'But your father has been forced to serve the resistance in an unofficial capacity. He's following the Organisation's orders. What exactly are you getting at? Come on Omar, aren't you ashamed of harbouring suspicions about your father? And Salim – Salim has never dabbled in politics! He just wants to have a bit of fun like any other boy his age. Did you know your brother's a marvellous dancer? And what about me? What do you think about me?'

The new photographs his mother had brought him depicted not only family members, but also the beautiful mosques, churches and synagogues of various capitals around the world that his grandfather had visited during Omar's absence. They also portrayed the enormous dockyards chock-full of interwoven structures and slumbering ships of various shapes and sizes. Photos of Geneva, Barcelona and Marseille (where, during the 130-year-long colonial era, they had made soap from the bodies of Algerians stolen from cemeteries), where Mr Baltayan, an Armenian living in exile in France, an inseparable friend and steadfast business partner of Si Mustafa's, continued to manage the buying, selling and grooming of racehorses in Europe. Nadia hadn't stopped telling Omar all the latest news ever since she'd burst into that hospital room in Moscow: Si Mustafa, her father-in-law, was as usual roaming the world like the ancient explorers and seafarers he never stopped reading about and admiring, always on the lookout for new mares and stallions to breed with his own. Si Mustafa had stubbornly resisted selling Fascination II, who had attracted the attention of numerous buyers who perhaps thought that, as Omar had left for the war, he would certainly die or quickly be captured by the French, quickly tortured, quickly sentenced to death and quickly guillotined, and that Fascination II's owner would die of grief. 'You know he's still involved in politics at his age! Can you believe it? That's the sort of man your grandfather is!' Nadia concluded.

Nadia's peculiar behaviour aroused Omar's curiosity. He knew full well she was playing the role of Mother Hen and steadfast wife, but he suspected her... Omar conjured up images of searing blizzards, sand-storms, Arctic glaciers, frozen deserts, slimy swamps, exotic foliage, Andalusian plains where splendid horses galloped, dilapidated African villages, Chinese workers smiling on their bicycles, young African girls, Algerian, Moroccan and Vietnamese prostitutes and so forth. Far away as he was, it helped him visualise the teeming world that entered the family home through Si Mustafa's famous photos, which frightened his wife, daughter-in-law and all the other women of the family, who were shocked by the outlandishness or erotic indecency of certain pictures Omar's grandfather was naïve enough to purchase without much discernment or attentiveness.

Si Mustafa was fond of scribbling messages on the back of these famous postcards that were of astonishing warmth for a man of his generation, who had been born into such a backward, puritanical and hypocritical society. Si Mustafa – who was the complete opposite of my own father, a feudalistic, polygamous and paedophilic bastard – often mailed photographs of the stallions and mares he'd bought, giving plenty of details, such as the date and place the transaction was made. To avoid any problems with the colonial censors, he wrote his notes in French, since writing in Arabic was deemed a subversive act; despite the fact that the numbers in the date – the day, month and year – were actually Arabic!

So this paradoxical, often obscene world entered that large ancestral abode, an estate Nadia continued to manage despite her son's departure into the bush to fight in the resistance and his being wounded eight months later. She bore this burden despite the rumours surrounding her husband Kamal and the malicious gossip about Salim, her younger son, who was criticised for attending too many Saturday-night dances hosted by French colonists. Despite the suspicions that Omar harboured about her.

The plane was now climbing.

Chapter III

OMAR HAD READ SOMEWHERE that a language reveals the ambiguities of its history. He thought this might also be applicable to a country – his country in particular. And he grew more disconcerted when he remembered that his father, the Police Commissioner, had imposed the use of French upon his entire family, despite the fierce disapproval voiced by his grandfather, the horse-breeder. This bothered him because he knew that his father was not and had never been a collaborator during the war. He knew it was more ambiguous and more complex than that, but his father's insistence on speaking refined French had always worried him, arousing his suspicions. All the more so since his father's physique was startlingly Aryan. Omar's fairly aristocratic family with its Turkish origins was not the only one to be visited by such doubts after the end of the colonial period. Its patriarch, Si Mustafa, was a wealthy landholder who owned a stud farm that was famed throughout the region – and beyond – for the quality of its Arab thoroughbreds, which routinely snapped up prizes at racecourses around the world. Thanks to his trade, which required him to accompany his horses or track down other rare breeds, Si Mustafa was a polyglot; but he only used French when speaking with the French, never with members of his own family, especially since his wife only spoke Berber and Arabic.

It was this linguistic and patriotic uncertainty that planted the seeds of doubt in Omar's mind about his father's role during the war, when he was Police Commissioner in Batna, the capital of the Aurès region and epicentre of the 1954 rebellion against French occupation. Omar had mulled over that idea about the ambiguities of language, constantly churning it around in his head, right up to this day at Algiers airport when we were boarding the flight to Constantine and I decided to put an end once and for all to his qualms over his past and relieve his guilty conscience. The flight lasted exactly an hour, during which time I would need to clear up all the confusion that had been eating away at him for the past thirty years.

Once we had sat down, he repeated, mechanically, almost casually, 'A language is nothing but the sum of the ambiguities that its history has allowed to persist.' It was like a recitative. A requiem. By dint of repeating it to himself, he had almost started to sing it.

'I've never found out who said that. It's genius!' he said.

'It doesn't matter,' I replied, 'but it's so lucid and accurate.'

'It's incredible,' he went on. 'It's true of all of us, our history, our country – which has often been colonised, duped, betrayed, brushed aside, invaded… It also neatly sums up my father. Watch your tongue though! He was never a collaborator, believe you me! You do believe me, don't you? I know you loved him… He was a classy guy…'

'It's true,' I said.

'What's true?' he asked. 'That history's ambiguous or that you loved my father?'

'History's ambiguities, above all…' I replied. 'Proof of it lies in your unending suffering, the hard times you went through… You haven't stopped ranting or beating yourself up about it since you got back from the bush… One might even go so far as to say that you take great pleasure in stirring up all that blood, all that mud, all that muck… Ambiguity! We're all caught up in ambiguities, your father too! After all, the war is over now, Omar. It's been over for a long time. And after it was over we messed everything up. We became just like the rest of them. All revolutions end in failure, but one still has to go through with them.'

The plane went through a patch of turbulence. It pitched to and fro, making Omar's body and face seem like they too were tossing and turning. His face, already pale, grew even whiter. It wasn't that he was afraid, but he had been thrown by what I had said to him in the heat of the moment: *Your father too!*

Omar fell silent. I felt relieved. We were silent for a long while. I felt the aircraft cut through the clouds, diving, then climbing back up, only to dip once again. It reminded me of the French army's small reconnaissance jets during the resistance, which we called 'Hornets' because they were invariably yellow. Invariably deafening. The war was horrible.

The plane continued to nose up through the clouds.

Throughout this war, we had climbed the mountains of the Aurès region, amazed by how quickly we had gone from being model students at an elite secondary school, where we were among the few Algerians, to being soldiers of the resistance, just like that – an amazement we put down to fear or bewilderment. It was as if some days these mountains would burst out from under our feet, appearing round a corner, suddenly becoming visible through winter clouds or summer mists – which were much denser and disorienting – leaving us stunned and dumbfounded. The trees began to spin around us as we walked, climbed the rocks and crawled on the muddy, slippery ground until we were exhausted, and then went beyond exhaustion into total breakdown. We were so tired and frightened that we had the feeling we were walking beside our bone-weary bodies, as if our stiff limbs were flailing disjointedly around us.

We always had the feeling that everything was stirring, closing in and moving in a halo in that scorching heat, deadly for those of us who were unaccustomed to its intensity, as was this mayhem of raging elements that were in actual fact perfectly immobile and static. This pandemonium of rocks and vegetation helped us pass by undetected, allowing us to be in two places at once and watch our shadows crumble under the effects of the heat or the cold. Those were long and tedious marches, where we walked, dazed and bruised, between the prickly pears, the jujube trees, the olive trees, the Barbary figs, the charred remains of Jeeps, disembowelled tanks, the fragments of shrapnel and the mines buried just under the scree that was sullied for miles on end with napalm and the blood of dead, crushed and stunned-looking villagers. The remains of B52 bombers dotted our path as if they had always been a part of the landscape, part of the necessary conflagration typical of this sort of calamitous war... But above all, we were frightened of those yellow Hornets, whose unexpected appearance scared us half to death when they flew so close to the ground that we felt as if they might land right on our heads.

We carried our ancient, outdated rifles over our shoulders and, despite the crushing pain in our chests, we tried to exorcise that cloying fear, to speed up our victory – inevitable on some days and impossible on others. Our hope had grown contorted with waiting, tiredness and the weight of our old-fashioned rifles.

We certainly felt next to no euphoria at taking part in this war, since we had very quickly stopped believing all the nonsense with which our heads were crammed. We were afraid. Afraid of everything. Of our ruthless adversary. Of our equally ruthless leaders. Of the natural elements, hostile and deadly. Of the heat and the sun. Of the snow and the cold. Of lice and crabs. Of this war of blitzkriegs, traps and ambushes, tears and all sorts of bodily secretions. Guts trailing from the puny, fly-covered bodies of our comrades and of French soldiers. Entrails vomited from mouths. Innards pouring out of the usual confines of the human body, teaching all of us who had not yet died where our limits were. Living in expectation of death.

War: that scurrilous feeling snaking through our nervous system – already on edge – oozing through our spinal cord, through tightening vessels, through the bones and vertebrae of our valiant comrades and our ruthless adversaries, stained with the ochre dust of a land that was both hospitable and unforgiving. Bits of brain splattering all around us, which we perceived through our tears and our streams of sweat, despite being blinded by these horrible calamities, by the excessively raging sun, the excessively blue sky, the excessively white snow, the excessively crystal-clear waters of the lakes, the excessive rain, the excessive heat waves and the excessive ice. Our list of grievances was interminable. Scraps of metal and bits of pointed lead hailed down on us like the rainstorms of our childhood. We were too young and when night fell some of us cried out for our mothers or vainly pleaded with our unyielding commanders. When the sun rose, so did our pride, and we became once more hungry for violence, for acts of military prowess, feats of arms, for giddying exploits of bravery and heroism. And always the feeling that the mountains were marching towards us! The exhilaration of vengeance? The cruelty of the slave that has rid himself of his bonds after a century and a half of silence, fear and servile compliance? Perhaps. But what of our old weapons? We had precious few of them, though when Henri Maillot, a communist *pied noir*, hijacked a vast cargo of sophisticated weaponry belonging to the French army and handed it over to a resistance unit, the Organisation's worries were alleviated for a while.

THE COMMUNIST TRAITOR HENRI MAILLOT HAS SEIZED A CARGO OF WEAPONS AND DELIVERED IT TO THE *FELLAGHA*

We were overwhelmed by these things. We retreated into the safety of blasphemy and defiance, always careful to forget all the redundant hyperbole forced down our throats during the daily raising of the flag designed to turn us into blithe, callous jingoists. What idiots! At night, we even lost faith in our compasses, whose needles were agitated by the magnetism of our flustered bodies. (Who knows? Perhaps Omar's mother had a point after all when she deliberately set the wrong time on those fabled 19 Sicilian clocks – that had once allegedly belonged to her ancestor, a pirate – so as to then spend her time fixing them and thereby stave off boredom. No one had ever laid eyes on those clocks, since Nadia claimed she had hidden them in a safe-box underneath the foundations of the ancestral home.) The constant hail of lead and the intoxicating smell of gunpowder made us complacent, and we banished even the notion of danger.

We had meanwhile become adept at determining our grid coordinates on our maps using the compasses hanging from our necks while lying flat on the ground. We were our own guides and knew our terrain inch by inch, furrow by furrow, gorge by gorge. Our nostrils turned into sensitive seismographs that flew into a panic at the approach of the enemy. We were wretched, indecisive heroes. We watched the riverbeds run dry after bombing raids and olive trees spin root over branch. Barbary figs exploded in our faces, their colourful thorns slashing our cheeks. Our patience was otherworldly. The wait was long. Our bodies were starved; our pride wounded. We had had our fill of famines, fumigations and immurations.

In a letter to his brother, General Saint-Arnaud, who took Constantine in 1836, wrote: 'When the Arabs held out against us, we fumigated and immured them in their caves like foxes…' A trail of epidemics, looting, torture and rape. All this colonial gesturing had to stop. The war had made the unruly mountains inch towards us, as if drawn by our rancour and rage. The caves, which we surveyed until dizzy with vertigo, had been transformed into a vast underground network whose offshoots spread through the whole country. On some days, we were so exhausted and panic-stricken that we even began to believe that our hiking boots were marching alongside us. We then came to understand what a state of constant dread the French soldiers must have been in, inspiring in us alternate feelings of hatred and pity.

We had entered the war in the same manner that one enters a steamy hammam when it's chilly outside. At night, during the few hours of rushed, intermittent sleep, I dreamt of the purplish breasts of sweaty women sliding between my legs; of Kamar, my young stepmother, barely a woman, and the debauched, incestuous, overexcited and utterly shameless twins that Omar and I had met some time before joining the resistance.

We had poisoned over-zealous guard dogs, cut the throats of *caïds*, shot some corrupt imams, iced some *harkis* who wavered between fear and arrogance. We had cried at the time of their execution, because we understood how hunger had clouded the judgement of these poor, destitute villagers, whose loyalties had been purchased by the French army. Having thus become bloody-minded *harkis*, they had failed to make any sense of the war, this sudden whirlwind heading towards them. Nor did they have any grasp of history.

We had crossed out the meaningless words, the speeches and demagogic rants with the tips of our bayonets. We were then taken to our leaders, who angered us with their smooth-talk, their unbelievably cruel punishments, their pointless chores, their attempted rapes, their little side-businesses, their conspiracies and the horrible way in which they settled their scores. We already knew that Abane had been murdered in a sordid manner by Boussouf on the orders, and in the presence, of Krim Belkacem. We knew who had massacred the 300 villagers at Mellouza. We knew about all the revolting atrocities that had been committed against the communist rebels at the behest of the Organisation and with its blessing… We quickly learnt that war was an inferno traversed by rivers of blood and vomit. Our entrails exploded in our hands, turned blue by the stings of mischievous flies.

Yet all these resistance fighters who carried out atrocities had the right to be wrong, to make mistakes and to commit crimes, because this Algerian war had subjugated them, driven them stark raving mad – to the point where they had given themselves over entirely to this revolution without heed to either thought or reflection. They had sacrificed themselves, were ready to die; abandoning their wives and children and throwing themselves into this hellish fire that was the war – that ferocious war that France waged in such a merciless, inhumane and pernicious way.

The colonial newspapers kept printing bloody headlines, as if to reassure the public of their successes:

200 *FELLAGHA* NEUTRALISED
IN THE AURÈS MOUNTAINS

Decked out in all their ribbons and medals, the French army commanders refused to come to terms with reality. We felt the phosphorescence as our bones de-calcified under our skin and we became impregnated with the pungent smell of gunpowder, the nauseous stench of napalm, the fumes of incendiary bombs and the stink of rancid wool. Those who had dismissed our uprising at the start began to have second thoughts: they began to pass edicts about anything that came to their minds: establishing military tribunals, sending reinforcements of men and weapons, handing out death sentences to the likes of Fernand Yveton, Ahmed Zabana and Mohammed Ferradj (fifty rebel fighters were guillotined during the seven-year conflict). Their murderous 'Operations' bore the names of precious stones – Topaz, Amber, Opal, Ruby, Sapphire, Emerald – or of chesty actresses – Brigitte Bardot, Gina Lollobrigida. They had all lost their minds.

I was so utterly horrified that I no longer had any erotic dreams. Kamar, my young stepmother, as well as the twins, Mounia and Dounia, were henceforth cast from my mind because they loved no one. As soon as I joined the resistance in my own right, one of the twins – how could you tell them apart when they were so frustratingly identical? – managed to send me a letter in which she declared her affections for me. I was taken aback, but I replied. A more-or-less regular correspondence was thus established between us. Dounia – or was it Mounia? – began to receive a flood of my clumsy letters. Letters I wrote to mitigate the effects of the frightening days and the terrifying nights. Letters I wrote to forget the incest I had committed with Kamar, my stepmother.

I took the opportunity to tell her about the bush, describing it as a wonderful place, in order to avoid saying that the real situation was anything but rosy. I was afraid of disappointing her, of dragging her into those boring, ignoble days that might impede her from living out her real life with a sense of adventure and spontaneity.

To make her think I was a hero, I therefore subjected her to an endless stream of my illegible, naïve letters, sending them whenever we came to a halt in our marches. I avoided talking about Omar purely out of jealousy, however much I tried to forget my own wounded pride. I never stopped rearranging the events I had lived through, bringing a tight, bolstered and unusual order to my experiences, welding one detail to another so as to leave no room for doubt. Above all, I was wary of falling into complacency, which would have spoilt my cool, detached way of calling things into question: all out of fear that she – Dounia or Mounia? – might discover that her lover had committed incest and had further compromised himself by his idiotic heroism.

Her replies were always concise, as if her brevity and restraint were her way of reproaching my incontinent rambling, which in actual fact I used to piece together the fragments of my past, as well as that of Omar – whom I idolised – carefully handling the fragile elements of memory in order to give myself, above all, a bit of courage. I nevertheless continued sending her these overexcited missives, despite her reticence, which I surmised through the casual, negligent tone of her replies. She only ever reminisced about the debauched times we'd had together in the company of her identical twin and Omar, who never found out about our secret little correspondence. (She only ever talked about sex, or desire, as well as the plans we could put into practice after the end of the war – 'Do you promise?') I'd never had the courage to tell Omar the truth about this secret correspondence right up to the moment we had boarded this latest flight together from Algiers to Constantine.

Between letters to Mounia – or Dounia – we continued to charge through the Barbary figs, strawberry trees and prickly cactuses set aflame by napalm, the sun and the splatter of fresh blood that coagulated in the blink of an eye. We held our breath so as to trap the ghosts of our ancestors that had crumbled into dust after turning to stone in the quagmire of the war. Another matter I kept from Dounia – or Mounia – in those letters was the inevitable settling of scores caused by the pride of some of our commanders. They were so thirsty for power and riches that they often naïvely fell foul of traps laid by the French. The Great Kabylia bush witnessed the murder of a great number of intellectuals as well as the massacre of hundreds of villagers suspected of collaborating with the enemy, actions carried out by Colonel Amirouche, a skilful military strategist, whose tenacity and courage were exemplary, but who fell victim to the psychological tactics employed by the French army's secret services, who called this conspiracy the 'Bleuite'. It was this very same Amirouche who had sent dozens of intellectuals and women towards the border with Tunisia in order to spare them, once the French bombing campaigns became unbearable!

We were on the edge, marching on while dwelling on our anger. We came out of nowhere, showering strangers with buckshot and explosive or hollow-point bullets before disappearing once again, leaving the enemy stunned and dazed. We pushed past our limits, crawling on the ground without any respite until the horizon began to buckle and turn into a web of mirages, which we would one day have the time to decipher. We clambered up mountain ridges to the rhythm of the swarms of the cactus flies buzzing around between us and the graves of those we had murdered.

The enemy soldiers spared from our spiteful vengeance gave us nightmares. We often dozed in mountain huts. We would wake with a start to find ourselves splashing about in the blood of our comrades, whom we buried with little ceremony before the vultures could get to them, so that their wounds would not fill with grass and soil teeming with worms. Afterwards, there was little we could do except play childish pranks on one another, affording us some relief from the usual pattern of violence, acrimony, resentment and deception. Sometimes, a furious blue flash whirled mercilessly through our minds. Doubt gnawed away at us. We felt weighed down by the empathy we felt for one another, as well as for our enemies. Omar's photo from the bush never left my side. Even though its quality was rather mediocre, it was my amulet, my lucky charm. My burden too!

And so we kept running and sliding down the slopes, while our dying comrades inhaled their last puffs of *kif* hashish, sucking it in until their final breath, before we buried them in miserable shrouds and scattered some quicklime over them. The days began to melt into one another and the nights overlapped, until we could no longer tell the difference between sunrise and flaming dusk, between sunset and the swell of emotions that unleashed our excitability and arrogance, enabling us to avoid the easy path cut by our ancestors at the beginning of time, when they too had taken up arms against their foreign aggressors and lost their wars...

90 *FELLAGHA* KILLED
IN THE GREAT KABYLIA
DURING
OPERATION GINA LOLLOBRIGIDA

...and who one after the other, distraught in the face of their defeats, had cornered themselves into dissatisfaction, into petty feuds, into compromises and betrayals, leaving the triumphant outsiders to wield the rights of death and citizenship over them, thereby clearing a path punctuated by fumigations and immurations, tactics employed to wipe out entire tribes. Omar was obsessed with General Saint-Arnaud's letters, which narrated all the genocides he had committed in such a cool, detached manner, all the while displaying such sentimentality when it came to the education of Adolph, his little brother, or to the death of Delphine, his little niece. Those letters were a chronicle of bloodbaths, massacres, burnt crops and confiscated farms.

The only thing left to us was to play tricks on reality, to outwit the enemy's maps, since we had inherited nothing from our ancestors: no tactics, no eye-witness accounts, no military stratagems; nothing at all that might have helped us bring their dreams of vengeance to fruition. Were we ungrateful towards these ancestors? No doubt. We were too intransigent, too clearsighted about the situation we'd found ourselves in. We were all too aware of past uprisings, rebellions and insubordinations, all of which had been etched on our memories thanks to Mr Baudier, who taught us French, Latin and Greek, as well as to Mr Ben Ashour, who taught us Arabic poetry; all of this didn't satisfy us. We were saddened by how many times our ancestors had been beaten. Were we certain of our destiny? Not really. We were so often betrayed by our compasses, our unspeakable fear and the palpitations of our hearts, which were gripped by uncertainty – why had the resistance slaughtered Mellouza's 300 inhabitants in May 1957? Why had Colonel Amirouche executed so many illustrious intellectuals? Why had Boussouf, the head of the Organisation's secret services, in cahoots with Krim Belkacem, had his brother-in-arms Abbane strangled? Why? 'Because it was the revolution,' Omar would tell himself over and over during the war. I, on the other hand, would say, 'Because they were misled by the conspiracies hatched by the French army's intelligence services.' But that wasn't the whole story! I know… I know!

Omar, meanwhile, was talking about his father and his younger brother, insisting on their complete and total innocence, but I wasn't listening to him. I was lost in the memories of that shameful, scabrous war.

The plane had now reached its cruising speed.

Chapter IV

THE ALGIERS–CONSTANTINE FLIGHT WAS full, and Omar and I were whispering, having a heated debate about opposing versions of the truth, delving into the darkest depths of our past. Our conversation was as disconcerting and as farcical as always. I hovered between sympathy and exasperation whenever he broached the topic of his father. Worse still, there was another painful matter of which he never spoke, but which was nonetheless always there, lying in ambush, behind his words, his silences, his sidelong glances.

What really weighed on Omar's mind was the disappearance of his youngest brother Salim during the first days of Independence; his body had never been found. But I said nothing. A stern, amorphous silence fell over us. He kept his eyes fixed straight ahead, as if staring – to the brink of light-headedness – at an imaginary point. But there was nothing. Nothing but the round heads of our fellow travellers – of all shapes and colours – which he tried to cling to. Nothing but the oscillations and vibrations of the plane that sped through the clouds or turned at a right angle from time to time. I was anguished by the thought that something thick had insidiously settled between us. I didn't want to speak because I didn't know what to say. He had immured himself in his silence. Retreated into himself. Sitting next to me. As if he were dead.

While Omar was sulking (which I knew would last for

exactly 15 minutes), I reminisced about our youth, the summer
holidays we spent at the house that belonged to Omar's father,
Uncle Kamal, or rather his grandfather, Si Mustafa, the unas-
suming but indisputable patriarch of the tribe. Omar adored
both his father and grandfather, and at the beginning of each
summer couldn't refrain from flinging open the doors of that
wardrobe, in its pride of place in that immense bedroom, with
such theatrics and arrogance – as if he wanted to stress how
much he loved his family and how proud he was that they
bought him such beautiful clothes and shoes. On one occasion,
the wardrobe's double doors had opened to reveal – in front of
my dumbstruck eyes – a plethora of suits, shirts, pullovers and
shoes. I was jealous of this vast array of luxurious clothes cut
from English, Kashmiri and Chinese cloths (the silk shirts).
Hastily slamming the wardrobe doors shut, I turned spitefully
towards Omar and said, 'Do you remember the history of the
French conquest that Mr Baudier taught us?'

He stood still. Dumb. His arms hanging loose. He stuttered,
'Yes… I think so…' I replied, 'You think so? You think so, or
do you actually know?' I then began to recite Mr Baudier's
lessons from memory in a cheeky voice.

5 July 1830: Conquest of Algiers by General de Bourmont
15 August 1830: Conquest of Oran by General Bugeaud
2 September 1830: Conquest of Bône by General Clauzel
14 September 1830: Conquest of Constantine by General
    Saint-Arnaud

Followed by an entire litany of defeats we should never
forget, at least according to Mr Baudier, Mr Ben Ashour and
Si Mustafa, who had then quickly gone on to speak about Lalla

Fatma N'Soumer's resistance in Kabylia (1830–1857); that of Ahmed Bey in Constantine (1830–1836), which had claimed the life of General Damremont during the siege of that city; and above all that of Emir Abd el-Kader at Tlemcen (1830–1843). When Mr Baudier listed those various rebellions, he would say, 'No, children, those don't count. A defeat is a defeat. You have to be conscious of that, painfully conscious, so as to be able to prepare for what's to come. The revolution is coming soon. Trust me children, but don't forget: a defeat is a defeat! That's all there is to it, and one hundred and twenty years later we are still reeling from that defeat. Too late, too late are we paying heed to Emir Abd el-Kader, to Lalla Fatma N'Soumer, to Ahmed Bey… but despite it all, I am a little apprehensive about Independence. One day you'll understand.' We were stunned, outraged even to hear such an exemplary patriot make such remarks. Shocked, but also captivated, and in a confused way, we agreed with him.

After the ritual display of the clothes, we would then go onto the large terrace of the house and begin our 'holy scriptures', which was the secret and ironic code-name we gave to political slogans. Omar and I would preside over the painting of these slogans, directing the efforts of the assembled cohort of his brothers, sisters and cousins.

I was tasked with coming up with punchy slogans, while Omar was in charge of supervising the quality of the calligraphy. The others soon covered the entirety of the terrace with slogans written in gigantic letters using large pieces of coloured chalk:

DOUN WITH FRANSE
LONG LIVE ALGERIA

From time to time, Si Mustafa would come and check the consistency of the slogans to ensure the spelling was correct and the calligraphy up to scratch. But he was just pretending. He was quick to ignore mistakes, the bad quality of the writing and the facile naïvety of the slogans. Because he knew that we made these mistakes on purpose in order to throw the French police and their Algerian spies off our scent. To mislead the enemy of course! He would utter only a single phrase – 'Very good, children!' – and then disappear to tend to his crops, his horses and his clandestine meetings, as well as the infinite hours he devoted to reading; spending the early afternoon summer siestas and the cold winter evenings alone, barricaded in a windowless room at the bottom of the house that was cool and silent in summer and warm and peaceful in winter.

This was during the holidays we spent at Si Mustafa's, Omar's grandfather and father of my uncle Kamal, whose tall frame and blond hair made him look Prussian. These holidays, which lasted the whole summer, were spent partly in the countryside and partly by the sea. It was the sunny side of the picture, a waking dream. The ancestral home that we lived in throughout the year in Constantine was the other side of the picture – a frightful inferno! To this day I am still appalled by the status my father imposed on us and jealous of how different Omar's family was. Two related families. Two completely opposing styles of life. Mine was in a constant state of commotion due to my polygamous father, who was fully occupied with his dozens of mistresses who were, for the most part, barely pubescent girls. Omar's family, on the other hand, was very tight-knit and harmonious, despite everything it would later endure after the war broke out.

My father ran a large retail business. He slept with reassuring alacrity. My mother was a repudiated woman. She would achieve her orgasms using her hand, or with the help of her cat, Nana. *Marabout*s were growing in number in our city. The attitudes that governed our society were feudal. Women had but a single right: to own and look after a vagina that had to be shaved daily. I was a precocious child. It was one of my father's lovers, a dancer, who told me that.

I didn't really understand what was going on. And yet I knew I'd done nothing wrong. I had merely watched this mistress of my father's undress, all the while thinking she wasn't as beautiful as my stepmother, Kamar. She had allowed me to watch her, adding, 'You're a chip off the old block, aren't you?' That too I didn't understand, nor what she was alluding to.

Omar and I attended an elite secondary school and, as such, were the pride of our families. Yet that was precisely why my uncles hated me, since the mere fact that I'd been accepted at the secondary school seemed to ensure my break with their class of rich, semi-feudal country squires. Kamar – which meant 'moon' – was very beautiful, but I spread a rumour that she was exceedingly ugly in order to make life more bearable for my mother. Every morning I went to the madrasah at four o'clock to learn my daily *surah*. At eight I headed off to the secondary school where I could dream a little, despite the suspicions that 'Quarter-to-Twelve' – the Corsican supervisor – had about me. He had been saddled with that nickname because he always stood with his feet at right angles. And 'Quarter-to-Twelve' was always on his feet, always lying in wait. Punctilious.

I had no love for the madrasah, and above all I hated the road in which it was situated; it smelt of linen that had been boiled and hung out to dry, of charcoal-grilled sausages, the sort my aunts said were made with cats' entrails. Rascal that I was, I ate them precisely for that reason: to have the soul of a cat and never have to die, since my mother had always told me that cats have nine lives.

There was a hammam on that road with a blindfolded donkey on its roof that went in circles around the well, forever drawing water; he didn't seem to mind, and since donkeys had no religion, the madrasah kids used to throw stones at it. I took part in this game only to allay the teacher's suspicions of my being a heretic due to the influence of my older brother Zahir, who was often seen in the company of a mysterious Jew. Our most common problem at the madrasah was how to doze while seeming awake; dozing was an art form. It consisted of never closing your mouth and keeping your balance, sitting still, like a baboon perched on a tree branch. As soon as we stopped yelling, the teacher's cane – shaped like a baguette and as precise as a homing missile – sprang into action. Once we'd succeeded in riling him, he would hit us indiscriminately with his cane: you don't mess about when it comes to religion!

I loved to doze in class in the winter and the teacher could do nothing about it since I was able to blackmail him. He had made inappropriate advances to me the year before and I had consented to them just so that he would leave me alone and allow me to carry on fantasising about Kamar's alluring body. Everyone consented to the teacher's advances. He stealthily fondled our thighs while something hard burned our rectal area. That was all! I knew it wasn't that big a deal.

My older brother kept an eye out for me at school. Omar didn't frequent this sort of school, but he gave me some advice. To tell the truth, Omar was jealous. He was in no danger. Everyone was afraid of the son of Batna's Police Commissioner.

My twin brother Zygote was always trying to pick a fight with me, argue with me and tell on me. Parents – who were generally apprised of such practices – usually looked away in order not to bring a man of God into disrepute. They were superstitious and didn't want to be subjected to the teacher's sorcery.

One of my sisters said that this was a throwback to the Arab Golden Age. Later, I learnt that poverty was what had driven the teacher to homosexuality, since one needed a lot of money to get married in our city. Women were sold for exorbitant prices, and whorehouses were simply unaffordable.

The school gates were painted green; on the inside, the walls were vermilion. We always sat on worn-out straw mats with our writing tablets in our hands and to rile the teacher we hollered so loudly it was as if there were 10,000 of us. The teacher would then get angry and start striking us randomly. Wham! The accursed cane whipped the air and struck our faces. We then reverted to an abrupt and total silence. Caught short, the teacher did not conceal his glee at having subdued us. He nodded his head contentedly. While learning our *surahs* we came across many words whose meaning eluded us and remained opaque. Some stories were amusing, while others weren't. They are all myths, my brother Zahir would say. He was a medical student, as well as an alcoholic, a homosexual and an atheist – I didn't have a clue what this last word meant.

On the street below, the old beggar women had already arrived. They quickly added their voices to ours until there was no telling whether they were asking for alms or reciting the verses of the Qur'an. As a result, we lost our train of thought and the beggars seemed to be perversely amused at the sound of our mumbling. The teacher didn't chase the beggars away. They too were able to blackmail him because he had made inappropriate advances to them as well, to which they consented as long as he gave them a few coins. It was both an open and a secret war that wore us down, something that made the teacher come, in every sense of the word.

The real war hadn't yet become a reality. But the massacres of Sétif, Guelma and Kharrata had already taken place. 45,000 people died in the space of a single week. It had begun on 8 May 1945, the day the armistice was signed between France and Germany. The Qur'an teacher couldn't have cared less about the Sétif massacres. He refused to get involved in politics. He said that it was not compatible with theology or with the principles of Islam. To tell the truth, he was a coward. Not even that. A vegetable? An invertebrate? Even he didn't know himself. He was an old man with cloudy eyes that had been ravaged by trachoma and conjunctivitis. He was rather dark-skinned and came from the south. He was very poor and wore some old rags on his back and had no buttons on his fly, though we nonetheless never saw his penis. He had no beard and his body was ensconced in an old *bournous*. He hung about there in the middle of the circle we had formed around him – the middle: that's where the power lies!

He became particularly fierce just as he started to get drowsy and wound up nodding off. We stopped dead in our tracks. The teacher was fast asleep. We had a sudden illusion of new possibilities. But the silence made us dizzy. Warm vibrations. A renewed sense of peace gave way to games. Voiceless dialogues. Charades. We laughed deep in our bellies like chuckling snakes. Fear gnawed at us and the proximity of danger added a bit of spice to our naughtiness. A fly-hunting party was organised and for a few maddening seconds we followed them, watching them land on the old man's swollen eyelids, anxiously waiting until they were within our reach – then wham! We caught them in our hands with a swift, gentle movement. The dexterity of dunces! We risked waking the teacher up, but took delight in being afraid. We were all worked up. As the hunt got more heated, we started taking more risks, ignoring all obstacles that stood between us and the flies. But all would be lost if the teacher suddenly woke up. A terrible slaughter of fat flies ensued, and we paraded them at length. Omar found the story of the flies most intriguing and wished that he too had taken part in our hunt. He went white in the face when I told him about these hilarious adventures.

We compared the insects and gave them flamboyant names, exclusively names of Berber kings and queens – Kahena, Jugurtha, Tacfarinas, Juba II, the Numidians – and of Roman emperors such as Nero and Caracalla. We held mock funerals and before killing them, we tried to train them to whistle, lisp and squeak… All in vain. When we had grown tired of our game, we gave the flies to a black child who swallowed them whole to impress us and extract some money from us. We passed the teacher's fez around to collect some money for the boy. We silently clapped our hands. All of a sudden, the fly-swallowing child mentioned his father, who had been carried off by *treponema pallidum* – Zahir explained to me that this was syphilis – which he had contracted in a sleazy Vietnamese bar. He cried and we took pity on him. Zahir, on the other hand, was unmoved: 'His father shouldn't have gone off to fight a colonial war in Indochina alongside the French!' Our first lesson in internationalism. On hearing our older brother talk about the war in Indochina, Zygote started to giggle. He had mastered the art of getting on my nerves. Omar didn't like Zygote either. He often told me, 'Are you really sure you're twins? That you are monozygotic? He's so different from you…'

In the end, the teacher woke up. The cane hissed like a venomous snake. There was no warning. The thick surge of voices was not out of the ordinary, the old beggar women were used to it. They understood what was going on and started to coo and yell abuse at the teacher. Once the teacher had woken up, the flies became brazen, reappearing in large numbers, having rummaged in the trash and then coming to sting our eyes, thereby certainly ensuring we'd catch some disease or other. The hour of salvation finally arrived. It was time to go to the French school. Seven o'clock in the morning.

I had waited impatiently for the summer, when I would be able to spend my vacation at Si Mustafa's – who had been arrested along with my father on 8 May 1945, a few days after the Sétif massacre – and meet up again with Omar, who loved coming to this large house in Constantine, where life, laughter and tears flowed freely. To be immersed once more in childhood.

All those adventures I had shared with Omar flashed past my eyes during the few moments of respite he gave me thanks to his sulky silence… 15 minutes had passed. Abruptly, Omar lowered his guard and, giggling as if to mock me, asked, 'How's Nana doing? How's Mozart?' My defences crumbled. He knew my weaknesses and could exploit them as and when he liked. Nana was my Siamese cat, who had the same name as my mother's cat. Mozart was my exceptionally gifted, music-loving hedgehog. Omar was the one who'd given him this name, and it suited him perfectly.

I replied, 'They make my being single more bearable. They're both fine. Would you like to see them today? Are you free this evening?' Of course he was. He didn't need to answer me. Omar said, 'Tell me, why did we stay single?'

The plane meanwhile seemed to have become motionless as it cruised through the peaceful, cottony sky.

Chapter V

ELEVEN O'CLOCK AT NIGHT. My mother doesn't want to look at the time. I am in her bedroom, sitting across from her. She is anxious. Zygote is sound asleep in the small room adjacent to hers. Zygote always sleeps soundly, indifferent to what is going on: the interminable wait for our older brother, an alcoholic, to return. This recurring scenario has always haunted me. All the pain my mother bore in silence.

'What time is it?' she asks.

'Ten o'clock.'

She's suspicious. She's always suspicious when it comes to the time. She's afraid I'm lying to her. As far as she's concerned, time doesn't really exist. And yet how can she feel such anguish if she lacks any notion of time? Despite this, my mother worries all too easily. It is her permanent state of being. With the exception of Zygote, no one sleeps much. The rest of the *smala* keeps its eyes on us. Our uncles are lying in wait, ready to mock us and bad-mouth Zahir and his Jewish professor. It's getting late and my older brother still hasn't come home. We wait up for him. I adopt a casual expression, but deep down I'm extremely frightened. My brother could have got himself run over by a car; he hasn't been sober in over a week. I softly mumble some prayers under my breath so as not to be heard. My mother is trembling. Nana, her cat, is curled up in her lap. But I feel that she too is nervous. The way the light is falling emphasises the fuzz on my mother's upper lip. One could say her moustache was similar to her cat's. She's so superstitious that she's holding back her tears.

The chair seems peaceful, as if located in the eye of the storm that is raging around us – how often it has sheltered and comforted us in this manner. The bed is very large. The ceiling panels are intricately decorated and are making my head spin. Everything seems enormous in that bedroom. I'm trying to let myself go and clear my head, but I feel anxiety surging inside me, growing like a white worm. The doorknob is round, white and particularly cold. I scrutinise it, but there is nothing to scrutinise.

'What time is it?'

'Still ten o'clock, Mother.'

'The alarm clock must have stopped…'

'You can hear it ticking!'

This sort of argument is nothing out of the ordinary. I open a book. The prayer beads click and their noise bothers me. She's gibbering behind her closed lips. All of a sudden, she strikes me as beautiful. She has some little wrinkles to the right of her chin, and since I can't see her left side, I come to the conclusion that she doesn't have any there. She's secretly counting the seconds on her fingers – is she aware there are sixty seconds in a minute? She's trying to verify what I've been saying. I have to keep one step ahead of her.

'It's half past ten.' I say.

I feel the urge to phone Omar. Ask for his help. Omar adores my mother, who is the complete opposite of his own, but it's too late in the evening; I think I'll call him tomorrow, or take the bus to Batna in order to see him.

She suddenly stops counting. She doesn't know what to say

and heaves a long sigh. It has actually just gone midnight and I'm also starting to worry. I suggest a word and try to get her to say it. I try to put her on the right path, but miss the mark. I am in the full grip of panic and this unexpected throwback to superstition exasperates me. I get up. Go over to the window. The street is empty. Cold. Filthy. Rubbish lies scattered on the pavement, as well as everywhere else. I sit back down. Mother gets up. She leaves the bedroom, and judging by her pace I can tell she is going for a pee. I prick up my ears: the liquid tinkles in the bowl. Pss! I have something resembling the taste of salt in my mouth. I'm sweating profusely. Is it uneasiness? I guess each move she makes, as if I were right in front of her. The vocation of us voyeurs! Pss!… The funny noise that women make when they attend to their needs. Bustling! She comes back in and sighs once more. The room feels cramped. It's winter. My mother is a saint. She never leaves her sewing room where she has buried herself under hundreds of bits of wonderful fabric that she transforms into dresses, kaftans and *sarouals* of exceptional beauty; all thanks to her sewing machine: an old Borletti she inherited from her mother.

I think Zahir's pushing his luck. Ever since the Sétif massacres in 1945, there have been military checkpoints and patrols everywhere. The French soldiers and their Algerian, Senegalese or Vietnamese auxiliaries are all too trigger-happy. They're dangerous, all the more so since Zahir is capable of goading and insulting them, especially when he's drunk. Why is he out getting drunk? He always says it is in order to believe in God. Omar teases me by telling me that Zahir is right. In fact, he even admires him and swears that when he's old enough to drink in bars, he will also spend his evenings there – in my company of course! As usual, Zygote is giggling. He's my twin brother and yet thinks I'm the elder because I was born three minutes before him. I don't see how this is at all relevant. Zahir is 20 years old. He's studying medicine at university and ever since his mother was repudiated, he has whiled away his time in the city's shady drinking holes. He drinks in the Spanish and Italian bars, but has a penchant for the Jewish bars, where they play LPs by Sheikh Raymond, the undisputed master of Constantinois Andalusian music. Mother is now in the full throes of panic and has started beseeching the Prophet Muhammad (whom my father is very devoted to and whom he loves spilling his guts to, omitting of course that one of his wives was only nine years old when he married her. After all, he believed he had merely been following in the Prophet's footsteps).

I decide I'm going to smash my drunken brother's face in as soon as he returns. Take advantage of his inebriated state. Alcoholic! When in one of his presumptuous moods, he's fond of saying how the world 'alcohol' is one of the many words with Arabic roots and that it's nothing to be ashamed of. He's very knowledgeable in that regard, and I can barely keep up. Zahir is a brilliant scholar. Before matriculating, he attended the Franco-Muslim secondary school – which Omar and I would later go to – where not even the ghost of a European would set foot, apart from the Corsican supervisor, 'Quarter-to-Twelve' with his club-foot and his habitual exclamations: 'Napoleon is full of shit! Arabs are stupid! Long live Free Corsica! Shut up!'

The ticking of the clock is so unbearably dull. My mother has taken up a position in front of the alarm clock and never once stops looking at it. I'm afraid. The latch on the door seems to have changed shape. I get up to touch it: it's cold. It looks different up close than it does from afar. That in itself isn't wholly disconcerting: it's the same with my mother's chin.

Like the breasts of the twins that Omar and I fucked every summer during our vacations at Bedjaia, by the sea: a mind-blowing spot. There's always a little difference. Mother starts counting the seconds again, but I no longer take any notice; she's out of it now. Her boudoir has no discernible smell; it lost its feminine scent after my father left her. Mother smells of nothing at all.

Nothing like Nadia, Omar's mother, who perfumes herself with essences that make my head spin. She's elegant and refined, follows European fashions and wears magnificent dresses and elaborate hats. She smokes Turkish cigarettes and drinks white Algerian wine. Just like French women. Moreover, she has a stunning beauty spot in the middle of her right cheek. That beauty spot never fails to arouse me. I feel remorse, but no shame. That's because of Omar. For a woman to give off a scent, she must perfume herself, whereas my mother smells of nothing but water. My mother is only desirable just after she's performed her ablutions, when her pores open up, attracting male attentions. What am I going to do? Should I go down to the street and start looking for Zahir? But where would I find him? One could drink at any number of bars of all nation-alities in Constantine, as well as in quite a few whorehouses. There were simply too many places to look.

'What time is it?'

'One o'clock in the morning.'

I regret those words as soon as I utter them, but by then it's too late. All of a sudden, Mother becomes aware of the time and starts giving in to her grief like someone possessed. She goes off in search of the incense burner to summon the dead, beseeching her ancestors to come to her son's aid. I start racing down the stairs, determined to find that drunkard wherever he might be. But there he is, curled up in the foetal position, his head resting on the threshold. I badly want Omar to be there so he can help me carry him up the stairs.

'I couldn't make it up…' he mumbles.

He stinks. He's writhing in pain. Mother hears the commotion. She comes down the stairs. Thanks to our combined efforts we're able to carry him as far as his bed. Mother goes out of the room, leaving the two of us in the dark. Zahir appears to be babbling incoherently, even though he's actually quite lucid. He's speaking ancient Greek. He really must be mad, I say to myself. My mother thinks it's Yiddish. I reassure her by telling her it's Aramaic.

'I was set on killing father… I went to the villa, but I couldn't go through with it after seeing Kamar, heavy with child, asleep in bed with him, the bastard. I just couldn't… I'd even borrowed a knife from old man Amar. I found flowers growing out of beer bottles in Amar's den; there was opium and *kif* all over the place. It was Father who taught me to drink, on his wedding night, that son of a bitch. Old Amar did well. I love him you know… he did well… but I would have killed Kamar and the child she was carrying… you can trust me… I don't care about the fact that you're fucking her behind everyone's back. I know all about it, Zygote does too… Forgive me, mother, forgive me… And you, matey, I know how badly you want to screw Kamar. You'd better hurry… because she'll soon be dead… I'm going to kill her… kill her baby… I'm going to kill that scoundrel! There was a flurry of voices in old Amar's den. Bleached-looking shirts. He wasn't alone, and his companions were laughing at my embarrassment. There was an opaque, impenetrable haze surrounding my plans… Fits of coughing under the smoky light shining down on the five people present. There was a wart on the groom's left eye. The horse was there, but it wasn't making any noise.' (That poor skinny beast, covered with festering sores, who bore it all with such patience that it still brings me to tears. It wasn't Fascination II. Oh no! She was a filly of exceptional breeding. At the slightest scratch they would send for the vet, who would take good care of her. He was German. Rumour had it that he was an old Gestapo officer who was hiding in Batna under an assumed identity.)

'During the days of Vichy France, the Pétainist *pieds noirs* organised several pogroms of Algerian Jews. Si Mustafa and our father – who were in regular contact with members of this community – gave shelter and sanctuary to a number of Jewish families. Our father was arrested by the Vichy authorities for this. It was one of the few times I was ever proud of him.

'The room was sparkling and whitewashed. I wanted to borrow old Amar's switchblade and go forth into my horrible night… towards Kamar's villa, to put an end to father and his unborn child. Amar offered me something to drink; I think I turned him down, but Amar – who is one of father's distant cousins (see how much you don't know!) – and his friends insisted so much that I wound up accepting. I don't remember a lot aside from their silly love songs and the chillies I swallowed. In their attempts to make me nauseous, they ground up some worms and began snorting them; I followed suit… I wound up arriving at the villa, but panic took hold of me as soon as I got there. I went back to Moshe's where I drank and listened to Sheikh Raymond records until they threw me out in the street.'

Zahir was often ill. When confined to bed, he would scrape the back of his throat with his fingers to make himself vomit.

He said that he was looking for his soul so he could get rid of it. He rarely went through with his threats. He refused to budge for whole days on end – always going on about how he was putting the Greek concept of *ataraxia* into practice because he was a rotten Arab who was in love with a Jew. To this day, I have never been able to make much sense of his ramblings and had little time for them anyway since I was so busy seducing my young stepmother, who was after all only my age! And who let me sleep with her whenever it suited her. To that end, I tried to wheedle myself into my father's graces, so as to obtain his trust. Zahir wasn't interested in women. He was in love with his professor of physiology, a blue-eyed, myopic Jew who often came to the house, despite my mother's obvious hostility towards him. I had nicknamed him 'Heimatlos', or 'stateless' in German, a language I was studying at secondary school with Mr Baudier, who was friendly to Arabs and who spoke to us about Algerian Independence in hushed whispers.

Initially, I thought being a homosexual was a mark of distinction since the Jew was strikingly handsome, had a sweet voice and was easily prone to tears. Each time I tried to understand my brother's relationship with his professor, Zahir would fly into a rage and yell at me, 'Go and chase after Kamar! Chase after your cousins! Go gossip with Omar!' Zahir and the professor had developed their own cryptic language in order to communicate with one another in the presence of a third party. The Jew often said he was not *heimatlos* and that he was Algerian. I didn't understand how one could be both Algerian and Jewish. Hearing this, Zahir would have another fit of rage and shout, 'You dirty racist!' I used to get so worked up I would have to run to the bathroom and masturbate. Heimatlos was very wealthy because his father had been a famous ophthalmic surgeon in our city and owned a state-of-the-art clinic. He was so devoted to his profession that he had gone blind. And yet some days I hated my mother's habit of cursing the Jews, even though to Zahir I was a racist too. To tell the truth, I knew very little about these religious matters. Our uncles did their utmost to keep us away from Zahir due to his doubly dubious friendships. As soon as the professor left our house, my mother would air out the rooms, wash the glasses the degenerate had drunk from and recite some magic spells. Despite the fact that she had given shelter to two Jewish families during Pétain's rule. Despite her friendliness with Henriette Gozlan, a Jewish seamstress, who would eventually become my father's third wife. Zahir kept a stony-faced expression and let my mother ramble on. He refused to explain himself, and as a result I grew more and more curious about this unusual relationship.

Sometimes Zahir would throw up a great deal, pull the bed sheets up to his chin and stay in bed staring at us without uttering a single word. Omar never stopped banging on about how he would one day be exactly like Zahir – that is as soon as he was old enough to start frequenting bars in Constantine. I pointed out that alcohol flowed freely in his house and that he therefore didn't need to go elsewhere. His rebuttal was 'Bars smell like people, like the poor. You'll see: they're the ones who'll chase the French out of Algeria in the end! The cocktails at my house are far too sophisticated for my liking…'

When things weren't going well with me, I would send Omar voluminous letters. I would tell him about all my troubles. I wanted him to compare his paradise to my hell. He had wonderful parents; friendly, tolerant and open-minded. My father was a miserable wretch who hounded and despised us; he was also very miserly, even though he was actually wealthy.

I had a brother who at the age of 20 was a brilliant medical student but already a chronic alcoholic. One day, I found a pile of his scribblings.

When I throw up, I feel once more the same putrid sensation I felt when I was ten years old. When I saw menstrual blood for the first time. Dripping down my mother's thigh. I thought I would die. I don't like throwing up, but whenever I think of blood, I can feel my guts rising towards my mouth. I am not feigning; I am actually ill. Once, Mother was sitting down and blood was dripping down her left thigh, quickly turning into a little stream on the floor. It was summer. It was exceedingly warm. Nobody said anything. For a moment, I thought my mother was going to die, but then she got up and ran off screaming. Nana, her cat, followed after her. I stayed there. Frozen. Pathetic.

Heimatlos is like me: he doesn't like menstrual blood either, and this is why I love him, despite his religion... Deep down, this need to vomit is no longer due to nausea, but to a lack of understanding; I throw up because I cannot see things clearly.

An image triggers my memory: I recall the more distant origins of my illness, in an orange-yellow haze. I am eight years old. The discovery of a bag containing blood-soaked rags behind the kitchen door. An awful smell. Between each crumpled piece of cloth, a gelatinous substance. The sun casting its blinding rays on the revolting bug. An aunt surprised me in the act and slapped me; despite this, I didn't want to leave without my orange marble, which had slipped in amongst the bloody rags. That day I understood that it was menstrual blood. And that is when I threw up for the first time.

Throughout my childhood, I dreamt of the rags stagnating in their filth, attracting a huge number of flies and insects keen on the feminine blood. I also dreamt that all women were dead, leaving no trace of their existence behind them, save for that awful stench. Ever since this encounter with feminine intimacy, I started to consider them as different, the purveyors of redoubtable dishes that attracted the cockroaches lying in wait under the kitchen doors. I nevertheless began to feel a horrifying attraction to those foul-smelling, syrupy fissures I saw swelling between our cousins' thighs when they let us stroke their legs right up to their vagina – which they always shaved – during our afternoon siestas when everyone slept out on the terrace. I was taken aback by the shape of their genitals and I beat a hasty retreat, preferring to watch the flat, smooth outline of their crotches from afar...

As for me, it was only much later, after I'd become an adult and started studying medicine (I chose this path as a tribute to Zahir, who died at the age of 20 in June 1956. Was it suicide, or had he been murdered by the French Secret Services or the Red Hand? Anything was possible!) that I was able to rid myself of the fears and prejudices that Zahir had instilled in me. He was wrong to think I should be deeply disturbed by all of this. He had sent me a letter because he didn't dare confront me in person: '*I never went further than caresses with Heimatlos; it was he who refused. He was peculiar at times. We were actually on bad terms, because this atheistic Jew claimed that the Bible was the greatest poem that humanity had ever produced; I put a stop to his enthusiasm by arguing that the Qur'an was far more beautiful. From that moment on, he abandoned anatomy for Arabic so he'd be able to compare the two. Mother can't have understood our relationship all that well. It would have been useless to tell her otherwise. If she learnt the truth one day, her goitre would blister and swallow up her whole pretty face. She might also have gone to bed with one of the* marabouts *she went to see along with Zygote, who would do anything for money, to ask for their advice. And to think he's your twin brother!'*

Omar rarely replied to any of my letters. He claimed he wasn't very good at writing, whereas the truth was that he was shocked by my bluntness and the prosaic manner in which I outlined my ideas. But I insisted on writing to him. He was my only buoy.

In one of his infrequent replies, Omar had tried to convince me – as if trying to distract my squalid imagination and to avoid answering my personal questions – that as soon as the French had conquered Algeria, factory-owners in Marseille had repeatedly stolen corpses from Algerian cemeteries so as to turn them into their famous soap. I didn't want to believe him. Later, Mr Baudier confirmed Omar's story. He showed me French newspapers of the time that related these events. There had even been a dispute between a member of parliament – a certain Ernst Briançon – who had demonstrated in front of the Chamber of Deputies and denounced these odious methods. The president of Marseille's soap manufacturers' confederation had replied in the following terms: 'By denouncing these attested practices, Mr Briançon has placed the entire soap manufacturing industry in jeopardy.'

My father's department store. Colossal. Deserted. The midday sun is at its height. Si Zoubir goes off for a long siesta, leaving me alone: there are no customers. Winter. A biting cold. The naps do my father some good since he suffers from high blood pressure. Too many stimulants, the doctors say. The waiting. The hope that something might come up. Nothing. A blank in my head. My mother also takes naps during the winter to help pass the time. The store is a mess. Account books. Invoices. The smell of ink and wood. Sunday: the colonists' day of rest. Lewdness. Flaccid penises. Things start to happen in slow motion. Women. They come in one at a time. They feel safe once inside the department store, and faced with a beardless brat, don't hesitate to remove their headscarves. I stroke my penis under the desk. The woman speaks. She is voluptuous. She asks for an item. Erection. I pretend not to understand so as to prolong our meeting.

The tenuous presence of women on the periphery of searing, twisted nightmares. Dry earth: not even the illusion of dampness. The urge to rape even the most decrepit and ugliest of women is but a side effect of the rage that hangs from my eyes, bulging with false desire. Outrageous perversity! The masturbating goes on all afternoon. Exhaustion. The unconsummated orgasm brings the image of Kamar, the young wicked stepmother, within range of my catastrophic desire. Each ejaculation leaves me feeling more crazed. The beginning of a slow death. A feverish wait, but nothing comes of it.

The same sort of anguish I feel when I watch my mother sleep: her strange breathing caused by a pulmonary oedema. The break has already happened; useless to look for anything further in it. A stretch of white wall; a ringing in my head. The same old solitude. Latent amnesia. The absurdity of déjà vu. The emptiness of gestures, of actions, of words that have already happened, captured by all my senses. Absurd! Joyless morning awakenings. Running errands for Kamar. Every morning I squint to get a better look at her satiny, fleshy thighs. She does everything she can to excite me. Wears no undergarments. Only a transparent silk nightgown, through which I can see her shaven pubis. She drives me mad. What should I do? My distress makes her burst out laughing. Zahir tells me, 'Why are you holding back? Why don't you screw her?' Omar is of the same opinion. But they don't know I have already slept with her and that the pangs of remorse are eating away at me!

Kamar's pubis! There's a queue at the fritter-seller's. A Tunisian. I take the opportunity to warm my hands over the cauldron of boiling oil into which the man is busy dropping the dough with delicate movements, despite his overwhelming obesity and the erosive dermatitis that makes his scalp itch. I tense up as soon as the fritter-seller speaks to me. I sense his underlying lust. Everyone knows he is carrying on a seedy affair with my brother Zahir. The man with the itchy scalp understands and doesn't press any further. Fritters for Kamar then. I watch her eat them. Sensations I only feel in the winter: boiling oil, sawdust, the mint tea the apprentices drink. Weight loss. Two fingers in the mouth... Bluh...! Vomiting. My nose is stinging.

A spiral staircase. A villa. Bountiful hospitality. Blood flower. She is stroking her tummy, leaning against the wall. Slut! What was it? Abdominal pain? Menstrual cramps? She keeps quiet. There is a heavy silence between us – isn't the tap dripping? To this day I am apprehensive about leaky taps – the water dripping into the sink glows in the autumnal sun. Two halves of a watermelon are lying next to the sink. The innuendo is clear. Nevertheless, there is a semblance of peacefulness. She munches on a large, squishy fritter. Her hands are covered in oil. She laughs at the allusion: oil, vaseline, fornication. She makes her slender hands dance in front of my child-like, precocious eyes. I can no longer contain myself. A few tentative steps. Then I run away. Zahir says I'm a coward. But he doesn't know the whole story...

I am dreaming with my eyes open: the whore in the yellow blouse. A classmate at secondary school told us about these sorts of things. He'd skipped maths class to go to the brothel. He told us everything. But he annoyed us when he stuttered right in the middle of the crucial parts of the story. We demanded more details. Why hadn't the whore taken her yellow blouse off? He didn't know. Did she have big breasts? Enormous! He also spoke of the oily vaseline in the big what-d'you-call-it. He didn't dare call it by its proper name. He slumped on the table and then cried out in joy once again. No one could concentrate on their work any more. We all wanted to go and ogle the girl and verify the stammerer's version of events... Omar didn't want to come with us. He said the stammerer was a pathological liar, whereas his father was a Police Commissioner who fucked European whores on the sly. What a hypocrite! I was fully aware of how Omar took the express bus to go and get a whiff of European women's armpits when their hands were raised to hold onto the bars. He only did that during the summer, when women wore sleeveless dresses.

My father's store. Noon, still. Siesta. At lunchtime, I sit down to eat some spicy couscous. With a lot of chilli. Fire in my mouth. Bowel movements will be difficult to say the least. The threat of red haemorrhoids like those my uncles have. I put my mouth under the running tap: glug-glug-glug... I long for a woman to emerge out of the bleak winter afternoon. One comes in and leaves. I masturbate. To and fro. Through the polished glass, I glimpse the shrinking outlines of passers-by. A child glues his face to the glass and sticks his tongue out at me. I was very frightened: his eye sockets were empty. Anticlimax.

The concept of death continues to grow inside my head. Lust stays intact despite the body's tiredness. A sumptuous boredom: I yawn. There are no customers. Should I go to sleep or fake an epileptic fit? Raise the entire neighbourhood. Make father start up in his bed. If I were actually ill, I might see more of him. I cough. It is a little less cold outside.

An old hunchbacked man comes into the store. He smiles weakly. He is poor. His nose seems to bend towards his over-sized ear. He is dragging with him a little brat who is so skinny he could have easily fitted in his pocket. That gives me the giggles! The child never once stops sniffling, but his father takes no notice of him. If only I could slide under the desk and surprise him: peek-a-boo! But the risk of the brat break-ing into uncontrollable tears is too great. No! Maybe an over-turned tram might make for a better distraction…

The child is mentally disabled, and people say that his father must have committed a heinous crime without leaving the blessed woman's sacramental vagina. An expression they mean to be suave. I am acquainted with the man's wife: a beautiful, matronly woman who sends him out to run one errand after the other. Buxom enough to feed all the neighbourhood cats. Her pink bra straps dig into her white flesh. An invitation to bawdiness? His wife is wonderful! I picture that vile man busily dribbling his slimy, lumpy saliva into her mouth. Wearing a turban. His beard bursts out like a manly growth on his other-wise soft, flabby face; the rest of his body is enshrouded in ano-nymity, but he certainly knows how to look after that beard!

A sophisticated bourgeois, who wears a greyish, loose-fitting *djellabah*. He has an undertaker's hands and sells candles. Since there are many saints in the city, business is going well. Com-petition between these saints is fierce, and they continually spread rumours and discontent so as to extract larger handouts from the colonial authorities. The man has a tiny shop. I love how shambolic it is. I often frequent it to smell the vials of musk, the bags of Javanese Frankincense, aloe vera and acacia gum. Hand in glove with the French, he is able to slow down the emancipation of women. He enters the shop. Ever so smoothly. Says something sweet or ingratiating. Damn him! The kid is capable of such obscenities that his father feels compelled to pull out his prayer beads to ask God's forgiveness. It will never end. Holding one's tongue is a primitive strategy!

Omar would often spend his weekends and vacations with me in Constantine, in that house where sadness always loomed over us. Omar held Zahir in great esteem and said that as soon as he'd gained his high school diploma he too would drink and be a homosexual, just like Zahir.

In fact, neither of us really knew what one was. Nor what it meant to be a Jew. Omar was a boarder at secondary school, where special arrangements had been made for him as a rich boy. His room, at the end of a corridor, had a shower, but he took his meals in the canteen, just like I did.

The plane still felt as if it were standing still.

Chapter VI

MEMORIES OF MY FATHER'S STORE. Again. Holding one's tongue is a primitive strategy – but one must use it regardless. This old man is one of Si Zoubir's most steadfast supporters and admires him for his many mistresses. He himself has to make do with elderly cleaning ladies. Assume an affable manner. The child is spruced up. His poor mother, I'm sure, must have spent a lot of time cleaning him up, even though he bears his stupidity as a blind man does his cane: people feel sorry for him. You have to keep an eye on that little brat! He has a penchant for telephones. (One mustn't forget that since my mother suffered from a goitre, I too might have been born a simpleton.) What should I tell the old man? That my father is asleep? No! That he's indulging his mistress? No! That he's nursing my mother through one of her attacks? No! Certainly not! He must never know about that. Degeneracy. He starts looking at me in a bemused manner. (Has he read my thoughts?) Charlatan!

By this time I am a student at Constantine's Franco-Muslim secondary school. Omar too, though he's cleverer than me and has skipped a couple of classes. Thanks to our teachers, Mr Ben Ashour and Mr Baudier, neither Omar nor I are superstitious. We have gradually become firm believers in the power of reason despite the influence of our extended family, who live their lives according to the sorceries and ways of the *marabouts* whose presence is a blight on our city.

The man who sells perfumes, incense and acacia gum is still there. Sitting. Immobile. The power of candles and the undertakers' evil spells. He has the same inspiring look about him as Sidi Amor, a Tunisian *marabout* celebrated throughout the Maghreb. Mother says that Muslims come to visit him from as far as India. On one occasion, my mother and I took the bus to Tunis in order to ask for his help in passing my diploma. In recognition of how serious the situation was, my father for once raised no objections. The *marabout* is a bedridden quadriplegic, a victim of syphilis. He lies enclosed in an enormous playpen, naked as the day he was born. His belly is three times the size of my father's. He's ancient and spends most of his time sleeping. He doesn't look at anyone and doesn't seem to be having much fun. From time to time, he emits a little war cry and gives way to his bodily functions. Then he laughs as if he really were a child. Mother speaks to him. He doesn't even listen to her. The invalid's family made a fortune by parading him around in his birthday suit, and the colonial authorities have discreetly encouraged this practice. His female visitors are the happiest. They adore him and feed him Syrian sweets, which they know he is very fond of. One has to pay a lot of money before leaving, but we slip away… Occasionally, and in return for a large sum of money, Zygote accompanies my mother to Tunis to go and see the *marabout*.

The man who sells perfumes and incense hasn't read my thoughts. That would have been the last straw! He must never know about my mother's goitre: to speak of a woman's neck is the sort of erotic talk that can spell disaster. Oh! Kamar… The effect you have on me… Reduced to being nothing but a longitudinal wound-licker – always that taste of salt in my mouth whenever I make love with the twins in Omar's company, or when I hear my mother urinate and when my female cousins let me watch. I'm exhausted. After all, am I not a lustful adolescent? I have the right to be left alone in peace! The women are immured, locked up in cramped conditions by the hundreds, suffocating inside those enormous walls so as not to awaken the lustful instincts of innocent men. Mr Baudier explained this to us. He's more politically minded than Mr Ben Ashour. Coming back from the hammam. Redness of the innermost depths. Washed, shaved and perfumed genitals. Right, I mustn't tell him about my mother. Everyone must think I'm a lunatic, but it isn't true. It's all just a ruse to fool that prick of a father of mine. Acting sweet, the old man looks at me. His son suddenly looks somewhat different from usual, yet I know him well, that kid! What does he want from me? I have another orgasm left in me. I start thinking of Kamar as she puts on her stockings – or did I lift that image from the silver screen? Zsa Zsa Gabor? Marlene Dietrich? Ava Gardner? Gina Lollobrigida? You only need to say something, recite some formula or other by rote, and hey presto. Avoid any slips of the tongue! The old man stays immobile, with a vacant gaze. He's unhappy.

A string of blessings rains down on me. The man regularly boasts of his mastery of the theosophical sciences as well as his wife and kid. He loves to chair political and religious meetings that are held in my father's office. He has no time for Averroes. 'He's an atheist!' he would say, spitting on the floor in disdain. My father is certain to catch us out on our knowledge of Islamic theology. We know sod all about it! Under the threat of violence, we are forced to take additional theology lessons to hammer it into us. Whenever he enters a room, he trails a sweet smell of camphor and burnt amber in his wake. Once an undertaker, always an undertaker. He's sitting, immobile. Like a fakir. But a malicious and double-crossing fakir. He asks after my father. I sense a trap and let him ramble on. As if he doesn't know! Everyone in town knows! Shall I tell him my father is brushing up on his French grammar with Miss Rocher, a nurse at Charles Nicolle Hospital? He might very well burst out laughing and start choking – that's how thin and frail-looking he is! Does he want details? His eyes light up, then quickly dim as if regretting the whole thing; his eyes return to the outside world. Lanterns! I would love to see him laugh. I bet he laughs like his candles.

I have the habit of going into his shop as a pretext to wander through the *souks*. The copper *souk*. The bitterness of the steaming streets permeated with the smell of orange blossom water. *Souk* el-Attarine where the pleasant scent of musk and benzoin overwhelms me. There he is. Away from his wife's pink bra straps and that horde of loutish children, he seems bigger, more full of himself. The eye sees more clearly. Silence. I let it last. To each the silence he deserves. It wouldn't do to offer him a coffee, since he might then take the opportunity to confide in me and I don't want to fraternise with such scum! His son is waving his skinny legs in the air like a grasshopper. He is suffocating.

'Lord! Give us this day our daily knowledge.'

I say nothing so as not to agitate him. He begins a sentence and, faced with my suddenly sarcastic manner, he stops short and starts to sulk. He comes across as a good-natured man, but is responsible for encouraging the head of our family to ask us trick questions about Muslim civilisation. ('Do you know how many hammams there were during the Arab heyday in the city of Córdoba alone?' – 'Err…' I have to buy myself some time. I assume an inspired expression to have a good think about it and instead opt to exaggerate. Go big: an astronomical number. My father's laughter chills me to the bone, while the candle-seller smiles at me condescendingly...) And there he is now, looking all bored, his prayer beads seemingly of little help to him. As if they disgust him!

'The flies...'

'Ohhh...' I reply.

He makes as if to move, then gives up on the idea. He looks at me and pulls a Qur'an from his pocket.

'May I read this out loud?... It's an old habit of mine, you see...'

The question is sly. This from a man who suspects me of being a disciple of Stalin! An atheist, a communist and a friend of the Jew Heimatlos! He doesn't even wait for me to answer. He reads (in a beautiful voice).

'No! Go ahead. Don't mind me ...'

While he's busy ranting, I turn my thoughts to that business of the soap in Marseille that was made with Algerian bodies. 'Those Marseillais are crazy!' I say to myself. I deliberately interrupt him. I tell him all about that horrible chapter in Algeria's colonial history just to irritate him. He breaks off. Looks indifferent. Blank. He quickly grows tired. I suddenly become afraid that my father has orchestrated the whole thing. Are they plotting against me? I need to find out the reason for his visit. I look at him. He's fallen asleep! At last, I understand: he has only come in for a quick nap. The kid is sat in front of the telephone, contemplating it with those puppy eyes of his. (You can bet on it!) I understand: his wife has kicked him out. I am the outlet for a domestic dispute. Jubilation! I picture her putting the strap of her enormous bra back into place. Let him have his nap and be on his way!

My father will be back any moment now. Glowing, despite his natural ugliness. His yellow, raw-silk *djellabah* and blue Moroccan slippers cutting a fine figure. I will then have to fetch him some fresh mint tea and some ice-cold water in an enormous earthenware pot with a bottom covered with tar. A ritual. The smell of the mint infusing in the scalding brew will take the edge off the undertaker's honeyed words and he will emerge from his siesta all clammy and agitated, his lamentable appearance contrasting with Si Zoubir's imposing bearing. Choking on his dreams. The first jasmine vendors make a thunderous entrance. The chap is asleep for the time being, his mouth open. His book has tumbled to the floor. The kid isn't looking for any trouble: he too will soon be fast asleep.

The telephone, what a marvel!

It was hot. Summer in Constantine was very hot. It was very cold in the winter and snow fell for six months.

My father was fascinated by history and often said, 'I can't say with any certainty why General Bugeaud, who was posted to the west of the country, was named Governor-General of Algeria. Was it a reward for his victory over Emir Abd el-Kader after an eleven-year conflict brought to an end by the treaty of Tafna – an agreement the General violated soon after? Or was it because General de Bourmont, who had conquered Algiers, had objected to the coup against Charles X and Louis-Philippe's rise to the throne – and had for this reason handed over his command of Algiers to General Clauzel? History has persistently failed to provide a clear-cut answer to all these questions.' Even Mr Baudier was uncharacteristically taciturn on the subject.

The fact remains that when Bugeaud became Governor-General of Algeria he instituted a vicious crackdown on the occupied country, killing a quarter of its population over the course of the following 15 years. Mr Baudier said that, according to the French army's statistics, Algeria's population fell from 3,000,000 inhabitants in 1830 to 2,000,000 in 1846. Zahir used to say that Mr Baudier was a left-wing Catholic who went to mass every Sunday accompanied by his wife and two daughters.

As it happens, I couldn't have cared less about all that fanfare the French seemed so fond of, but admired Mr Baudier's honesty and courage as he praised the example of Henri Maillot, an Algerian communist worker who knew where his real allegiances lay even after he was drafted into the French army.

THE CRIMINAL COMMUNIST CORPORAL
SETS UP THE RED REBELS
IN THE ORLÉANSVILLE AREA

Omar also didn't give a shit about any of the real or supposed reasons that had brought about General Bugeaud's rise to Governor-General of Algeria. But he never stopped reading the General's correspondence: the letters the General sent to his officers or members of his family. Omar would select passages from these letters and read them out to me, gushing over the elegance of the General's prose. I found it hugely exasperating. One of Bugeaud's phrases has ruined and haunted my life. Omar sent it to me from Batna one day while I was in Constantine. When I opened the envelope, there was just a slip of paper on which he had written this horrible sentence:

From General Bugeaud to General Pélissier.
If those Arab scoundrels retreat to their caves, take a page out of
Cavaignac's book, my friend! Do as he did to the Sbéas tribe: smoke
them out like foxes! I hope all is well with your family.
My regards to your wife.

I resented Omar for sending me this quote without any accompanying comments, without a single indication of the disgust, rage or horror that he might have felt at reading it. The incongruous blend of styles. Mind-blowing. That is to say, human.

Bugeaud's wording was clinical. It was also the way Omar behaved. A few years after this incident, during the summer holidays, he did it again by sending me a note on which he had written: 'According to the Larousse Dictionary, "smoking out" is a specific type of massacre.' Ever since, I have argued with him about these cynical, abject and perverted notes of his. Unspeakable, indeed! In fact it was the complete opposite. Omar's only intention was to instruct me on the horrors of colonialism, but his way of doing so was distinctly off-putting.

I decided never to open Omar's letters again, but I often went to see Mr Baudier at his home to verify these allegations. He always confirmed Omar's stories. Once, when I was on the verge of leaving his house, he added, 'The term "smoking out" really is in the dictionary, but not "immuration"! That should also be in there. The honour of all French people is compromised by its omission. Never forget that! "IMMURATION".' He spelt out each letter and I left feeling sick and disgusted and full of hate towards Omar. It was too hard to swallow. As a result, I also began to resent Mr Baudier and Mr Ben Ashour, the professor of Arabic poetry, who was rather keen on his drinking and who spent his time provoking 'Quarter-to-Twelve', the Corsican supervisor.

I was aware of the existence of the letters these colonial generals had exchanged with their families, but I had never suspected them of containing such monstrosities. So it was that General Pélissier invented the 'smoking out' technique. On 18 June 1845, he massacred more than 1,000 members of the Riah tribe in the Ghar El Freshish cave, located between Ténès and Cherchell. In August of that year, Pélissier faced some stiff competition from General Saint-Arnaud, who wrote: *I smoked out 500 of those crooks in a cave near Tipaza! You must follow suit! It's much faster…*

After hundreds of such occurrences throughout Algeria, General Bugeaud was subpoenaed by French Deputies who were horrified by his methods. He then stood in front of the Chamber of Peers in April 1846 and declared, 'I accept all responsibility. And I am further of the opinion that respect for human rights would only prolong the conflict!' Later still, during one of the flights we had taken together from Algiers to Constantine – or vice versa – Omar had told me, 'What you don't realise is that long before he smoked out thousands of Algerians, Bugeaud had been a real butcher in France too, slaughtering all the inhabitants of the Transnonain neighbourhood of Paris – now known as Beaubourg – during the 1834 uprisings, which began when a soldier was killed by a shot fired from a window. Immediately after the massacre, Bugeaud was dispatched to Algeria along with Cavaignac, the leading authority on the "smoking out" technique…'

That day, I was so angry that I said, 'In that case, why don't we talk about your father? And your brother?'

Taken aback, Omar said nothing. But there was a look of

pain in his eyes such as I have rarely seen in another human being.

It was around the time we were nearing the end of our university studies and taking the first steps in our careers. We had a passion for Constantine: the city of our teenage years and of our first depravities in whorehouses with bizarre, common names like 'The Black Cat', or 'The Moon'.

Constantine is still there, perched on its rocky plateau, with its dizzying hanging bridges across the ravines of the River Rummel that were a lure for the suicidal and swung on windy days. Constantine, with its superb kasbah, its teeming streets, its kebab vendors and the rams' heads being grilled on hot coals. The plane draws closer and from afar one can spot the city's ancient walls, aged, crenellated, large parts of it destroyed, with the Roman aqueduct snaking through the snow-capped mountains to make a brutal landing in the fertile Sétif plains.

The city resisted the invaders for seven years. One after the other, numerous French generals made attempts to take the city, all of which ended in failure. The first was by General Vallée, under the orders of General Saint-Arnaud, who oversaw the operation in the east from his base in the centre of the country. Faced with General Vallée's failures, his commander came to his assistance, but Ahmed Bey, the master of the city, was able to hold out. Saint-Arnaud wrote to his brother:

29 September 1837

Dear Brother,
We must at all costs conquer the city, which we know is rich in supplies, since our army is hungry and exhausted... But we are pressing on with our plan to capture it. Do not concern yourself!

All is well. The fate of our brother Adolphe must be decided. Both at his examinations and at secondary school. Let me know how he fares. I received a letter from our mother announcing the death of our great-niece, who joined her father in the afterlife fifteen days later. Do not forget to announce my appointment as head of the army in Constantine to our friends... These few lines, brother, written on my lap in my bivouac, are to inform you as to what has become of me and prevent you from worrying. I have a magnificent landscape in front of me. A thousand men camped out around Constantine. An unforgettable headquarters. An immense thing. I am concentrated, in my element. I will not attack on Friday 13 October, and will wait for Saturday 14. It's for the best!

It seems the brave General was superstitious!

And so, on Saturday 14 October 1837, General Saint-Arnaud attacked Constantine, which he was able to conquer thanks to the complicity of city notables whom he had bribed: Caïd Hamouda and Caïd Ferhat. Caïd Ben Gana refused to surrender and fled towards Biskra.

I said to Omar, 'You realise that while he was killing thousands of people he was also preoccupied by his younger brother's studies, and was above all struck by the death of his great-niece! It doesn't make any sense. You know, Omar; Bergson – whom you wrongly filled my head with! What sets man apart is not his capacity to laugh. Far from it... it's his cruelty!'

He replied, 'You already said that to me a long time ago, when we were still at secondary school in Constantine. I have come to agree with you over time! You were mature beyond your years... You were in year 11, while I was in the sixth form.'

On 20 October, Saint-Arnaud, that unrepentant hack, wrote a long, gushing and detailed letter to his brother about the conquest of the city. He was in the throes of ecstasy and jubilation. After bragging about his exploits, he added: '*The city was devastated. But, little by little, the shops re-opened. The Jews were out in force, in that chuckling, servile way of theirs, while the other inhabitants, the Arabs, were gloomy and grief-stricken. They shot us hateful looks. How could those people ever forget the pillaging of their homes and the destruction of their city? Not for many years.*'

By 1851, only 14 years later, General Saint-Arnaud had already forgotten all his regrets during the conquest of Constantine. He went on to crush the Kabyle uprising with undue ferocity, and, always in that gushing manner of his, wrote to his brother:

Jijel, 21 November 1851

Dear Brother,
I have just put up a cash bounty for every severed head and it has yielded excellent results in wiping out the Kabyles. We have wreaked havoc, burnt, pillaged, destroyed homes and trees. Even the Barbary figs haven't escaped our vengeance… Frankly speaking, brother, Algeria simply loses its poetry without massacres and smoke-outs.

I never stopped trotting out these stories to Omar – having got them from Mr Baudier and his drinking buddy Mr Ben Ashour, who dealt them out throughout the entirety of my time at the Franco-Muslim secondary school in small, gentle morsels, as if trying their best not to traumatise me. They trusted me. But not Omar. Because of his father's profession? Without a doubt. I tried to defend my favourite cousin. To no avail. Mr Baudier – who was kept under surveillance by the Red Hand, an offshoot of the French Secret Services whose role was to assassinate Algerians of French origin who sympathised with the idea of Independence – kept telling me over and over again, 'Omar is still the Police Commissioner's son. Never forget that.'

Mr Baudier taught me my first lessons in humanism, planting the seeds of a political conscience in me. He was a practising Catholic. During the war, the Algerian Church was progressive, anti-colonial and very close to the poor. This continues to this day. Monsignor Duval, the Archbishop of Algeria and Africa, was hated by the *pieds noirs*, who dubbed him 'Mohammed Ben Duval'. Mr Baudier was proud to belong to that church, whose point of reference and guiding symbol was not Saint Augustine – born in Thagaste (modern-day Souk Ahras) and Bishop of Hippo during the 2nd century AD – but Saint Donatus.

Omar explained the philosophy and praxis of this church, stressing that the Donatist sect was born in 3rd century Batna, the city where his father was Police Commissioner. Omar never stopped reminding me that Saint Donatus was born in that city, and took great pride in expounding the doctrines of Donatism, which he labelled a sort of primitive communism. He didn't have much time for Saint Augustine – whom he likened to a *harki* in the pay of Rome and its gentry – or the sentimental gibberish of his *Confessions*. My thinking wasn't far removed from his, but I thought he overdid it a little. It was as if, in his eyes, this Catholic, revolutionary, Donatist doctrine, which had long prospered in his native region, could rub out his father's dubious role as a double agent during the war, an experience that had eventually driven him mad when the country gained its independence.

Omar was looking for any excuse whatsoever to clear his

father's name and wash away the stain of his brother's crimes. Salim had joined the ranks of the OAS with such verve, spite and conviction, and been one of those who blew up the city's largest Moorish café in broad daylight, causing the death of hundreds of innocent people – right on the cusp of Independence!

By dredging up all these events, which he had never stopped mulling over, Omar had for the first time admitted that he had joined the resistance in order to make up for the crimes committed by his father and his younger brother. Furthermore he added, 'But when the Organisation decided to assign the attack on the Stade de Colombes to another agent, I felt betrayed, abandoned, cast back into my doubts, my sense of blame and my confusion. Why was the Organisation suspicious of me? Because of my father? It merely rubbed salt into the wound.'

'No, the Organisation wasn't suspicious of you! It perhaps even wanted to spare you a setback! After all, the Organisation sanctioned your return to the country and let you rejoin the struggle, right where Saint Augustine was born!'

Omar shook his head doubtfully.

It seemed as if the plane were hovering in mid-air.

Chapter VII

THE WHOLE OF ALGERIA was in the grip of war, and the Organisation decided to take the struggle to France. On Sunday 26 May 1957, the Stade de Colombes hosted the French Cup final between Toulouse and Angers. One spectator kept glancing sideways. Amidst the carnage of war, the Organisation decided to strike back. After a number of shimmies, passes and shots, the ball found the net nine times. Final score: Toulouse: 6 – Angers: 3. An underground operative's journey is about to make its mark on the newsreel. The Organisation was an impenetrable and strictly disciplined network of under-cover agents and assumed identities, all neatly encased in a pyramid structure: impenetrable and therefore indecipherable. Deep down, our collective past has always been in the throes of turmoil, subject to unpredictable factors and the randomness of luck; a tangle of trials and errors.

FC TOULOUSE: 6
SCO ANGERS: 3

The terrorist was anxious. He was too far from his target. He had been promised a place in the VIP stand, but had only been given a seat in a corner. Something had gone wrong. Besides, he shouldn't have been entrusted with the mission in the first place; the task had been intended for a certain 'Joe', a student.

What had happened? Had Joe lost heart at the last minute? Maybe he was the one who had the ticket for the VIP stand... Maybe...

To pass the time, or to muster a little courage, he hummed an Andalusian tune that had popped into his head, reminding him of Raymond the Jewish singer, who had been executed by the Organisation because they suspected him – completely erroneously – of being an informer. A total mistake. But it was during the war. He had every one of his albums. A shame! But Sheikh Raymond had been warned three times: an example needed to be made of him. Mown down point-blank, a tune still on his lips. The orders were strict, the people went into mourning, the song petered out. Even the birds no longer cried at twilight. The Organisation ordered the whorehouses to shut their doors. The pimps were brought to heel. The prostitutes made to take the veil. Alcohol, *kif* and cigarettes were forbidden. Steely discipline. Had Sheikh Raymond been showing off? He had counted on his popularity. Nothing could be done for him. The rules were the same for everyone. All death sentences – dealt out after three warnings went unheeded – were carried out without hope of reprieve... That was why Mohammed Ben Sadok, a plumber by trade, found himself in that over-crowded stadium. Collateral damage of the revolutionary war... All that remained of Sheikh Raymond, after he was reluctantly executed, was his voice. A state of war. A state of siege.

The Organisation had therefore decided to take the struggle to France. That was when Omar broke off his architecture studies in Aix-en-Provence and joined up. He was champing at the bit. Wanted to be put to the test. (To clear his father's name? Whitewash the shame caused by his collaborating with the enemy? Omar had no idea. And neither did I! All of the above contributed at least in part to his enlisting in the Organisation. But he was so mixed up! It was time to take action. Or else he would ask to be sent back to Algeria and dispatched to the bush. He wound up being chosen to assassinate Ali Chekkal during the French Cup final at the Stade de Colombes on May 26 1957. But something went wrong. He was replaced at the last minute by another activist, a simple plumber. Omar was the man behind that pseudonym, 'Joe'.)

Entire generations were sacrificed... Only death and dreams are to be found at the end of a song. The plumber was comfortable about his position, telling himself, 'I had nothing against Sheikh Raymond and had no hand in his downfall, and I have nothing against this *bashagha* twat either. He may even be a nice man, but he has bet on the wrong horse and is being stubborn...' Was Ali Chekkal a villain or simply a puppet? He didn't know. A ripple ran through the crowd. The scoreboard lit up and, as if by magic, 1 turned into 2. Toulouse: 2 – Angers: 0. Why not be happy, after all? He knew he was doomed, that he would be arrested, tortured, sentenced to death and guillotined! What to do now? He couldn't fire from such a distance. He must wait. Wait and watch the multitude of colours. The weather wasn't this pleasant every day in Paris, this magnetic metropolis that had partaken in the plunder of the world, while the colonists in Algeria hadn't even had the vision to be master cathedral-builders. The little plumber was an educated man. He took evening classes at the free university.

For example: the station in Bône, where he was from, was a pitiful mess that looked like a cross between Sudanese architecture and a New York skyscraper. The choice lay between laughing, laughing hysterically or bottling up rage – or giving in to fear. All these reactions were swept aside by the sound of voices, woodwind instruments, cymbals and clapping hands. The madness of the orchestra and the supporters' chants was a gelatinous atmosphere where human savagery was left to roam free. Some men cried. Some women fainted. Yet he was calm! But his impatience and feverishness grew with each passing moment, and as the details of the plan began to take shape in his head, he started going over the steps he must take, spelling them out to himself. Aside from the obvious historical implications that had made him both a master and a slave, the plumber also accepted having to put up with the roar of the crowd, chanting words he couldn't understand and that had nothing in common with his own language. He needed to get to grips with the facts. What day was it? (Sunday. 26 May 1957.)

The wait. And yet he felt a fatal love of life coursing through him. Everything else was nothing but a hollow choreography around a snitch – Ali Chekkal – who had been catapulted to the heights of prestige, decorated with thousands of medals, bought for fabulous sums and paraded in public with Republican pomp as if he were a mummy. Fossilised. Mineralised. Senile. Moronic. Inexorably heading towards his end like those beetles that die by getting their legs stuck in their own slime.

Mohammed Ben Sadok was fully aware that he would be arrested and executed after the assassination. There was no chance of escape! He could not stop thinking about all those who had been guillotined before him.

He – the terrorist who had replaced Omar (alias 'Joe') to murder Ali Chekkal, the *bashagha* – was still too far from his target, but he kept one eye on the field and the other on the VIP stand where he was now and again able to see the torso of the man he was meant to kill – depending on the movements of the officials who were sitting in their gilded rococo arm-chairs, which had red velvet seats, who, from time to time, leant fawningly towards the head of state, whose face was half hidden by the enormity of his wife's hat. The hat had endless brims and was fitted with a small veil and a ribbon that was tied in the shape of a bird or a flower or a feather – in any case something whimsical that he couldn't clearly make out from such a distance, especially since his view was partially blocked by the voluminous hairdo of a young woman who was sitting at an odd angle, and by the rolls of fat on the neck of an athletic-looking man, seated behind the armchair of the main guest of honour at this formal but antiquated assembly, who looked somewhat pointless and was almost certainly a bodyguard. But who was guarding whom? A French Republic heading for collapse, all thanks to the Algerian war…

Then he heard the man next to him yell while the rest of the audience held its breath, undoubtedly because one of the teams had a scoring opportunity; but the plumber was no longer looking at the field and was instead focusing his gaze on the VIP stand, which was jam-packed with senior officials and military officers, weighed down by their medals and their sense of authority. Alongside them were old ladyships withered by the storms of the centuries they had lived through from begin-ning to end, and beautiful women with tanned, naked backs who were surely bored to death, but were also clearly titillated by their proximity to all this power and money, their pres-ence in the corridors of power, where they had come with their spouses to play the role of trophy wives, of decorative plants, of shiny, luxurious objects, allowing their sharp-toothed, toupée-wearing husbands to make a name for themselves in diplo-matic, government and business circles…

The terrorist was wondering what could push a man to betrayal, or better still, what could push someone to refuse to do it and set himself up as a paladin of justice – and was then suddenly seized with a desire to explain himself, or rather to get a clear perspective on all of the acts he was going to commit and the moves he had predicted and analysed before putting his plans into practice.

Or to find some verbal expression for the vague scheme that he must carry out at any cost, as if he were afraid to find himself – before the gunshot struck the temple of that poor human thing wrapped up in his loose-fitting clothes and rough woollen *bournous* – confronted with an apprehension that had nothing to do with fear, but rather with the idea of firing a bullet from a revolver into a target immersed in a crowd of 43,125 spectators, a few hundred officials and their guests, a few dozen of the Organisation's agents, 22 players, the referee and two linesmen – not counting the inevitable gatecrashers, who are far more numerous at this sort of occasion than we might first imagine, and all in a stadium where the security services were out in force and all exits were heavily guarded. By the time this was over, all that would be left in his soul would be lingering dream-like traces of events that he would no longer be able to piece together.

That is, unless all these thoughts were just his attempts to reassure himself – he hoped that once he had assembled them into an interior monologue, his own words, the sheer scale of what he was about to do would swell to huge proportions and become a thing in itself, independent of his gestures and move-ments, leaving him alone. His small body was worn out by his plumber's work, his skin chafed by the heat of the blowtorch; he wanted to expectorate all the violence that had accumulated inside him, not since the start of the rebellion or his enlisting with the Organisation's saboteurs, but from a long time before that – ever since his childhood, or perhaps even before that, before he'd understood that he was an exile in his own country, living on the fringes of his own shanty town, a reject of colonial society, whose aberrations exasperated him to the point where he felt obliged to leave his native country behind and emigrate to France.

The summer dusk was closing in, long before nightfall and the end of the first half of the match. It was only 5:12 pm, the 23rd minute of play. The score hadn't changed – Toulouse 2 – Angers 0 – and the athletes kept on running back and forth across the pitch. Meanwhile, the plumber had sunk into a state of paralysis, to which his malnourished life as an exploited worker had no doubt contributed. Sunlight was flooding the steps, blinding him and preventing him from getting a good look at the grandstand. He was trying to muster all his energies, consciously channelling them towards the act he was about to commit, which had now been broken into a very precise and consistent series of steps, detailed down to the smallest gesture – leading him, despite himself, towards a killer's ultimate ecstasy.

Despite his disorientated state of mind and the fear he was experiencing, he continued to operate in a discreet, lucid manner, as if he had steadied his body with the sort of lead-like equilibrium that one usually tries to store away in the deepest depths of the mind.

He was nonetheless sure that the old man – the podgy, ugly, tubercular, horrible *bashagha* – would never regain consciousness, nor witness the proof of his passing, tattooed forever on his temple – if he did indeed go through the usual stages of coma and the inevitable death throes. Meanwhile, the score remained unchanged. Out of the speaker of a nearby transistor radio came a grating voice repeating that the score was unchanged and that FC Toulouse was leading by two goals to nil. Goals scored: the first in the 11th minute and the second in the 24th minute, both by Dereudre (Number 8).

While accomplishing his task, while shooting down the *bashagha* Ali Chekkal, while being arrested and condemned to death, the plumber never stopped thinking about Ahmed Zabana, the first resistance fighter to have been guillotined – or about Fernand Yveton, the communist militant who was executed on 6 February 1957 – the same day Omar had enlisted in the Organisation in France.

Omar had read through all the sport newspapers of the day that had covered the match. He had never admitted to being 'Joe', the man who had originally been entrusted with the assassination at the Stade de Colombes. He was sitting next to me on the plane. He was sulking. So was I. After a while, to lighten the mood, I said, 'Hello Joe!' His smile lit up his face.

He said, 'I lived under that alias for a whole year in Aix. And I was quite proud of it...'

'Joe! Pretty name, no?' I said, 'Sounds a bit Bronx, don't you think?' He burst out laughing. I saw his eyes well up.

The plane raced through the atmosphere like a giant, voracious, insatiable bird...

Chapter VIII

I WAS PERFECTLY AWARE that Uncle Kamal, Omar's father, had never been a collaborator. Not really. Yet when I ventured to say so, his son, who was brimming with spite, asked, 'What does that mean "not really"? Was he or wasn't he? In these circumstances, there can be one answer. And one only!' At which point I said, 'He was tossed about by the winds of history. He should have taken a stronger stance, and turned down the Organisation when they asked him to remain in his post and provide them with intelligence, weapons and men. He should have resigned and gone into the opposition. Just like you did when you were assigned that assassination at the Stade de Colombes, when they gave you that funny alias 'Joe'! Your father thought that being caught between two stools would be easier! And that's where he made a mess of it... And on top of that, where did all that money come from that he spent freely on himself and on you and Nadia? It certainly didn't come from your grandfather, did it? After all, he was despoiled and went bankrupt at the beginning of the war. He was a true rebel... Do you remember the wardrobes you flung open in front of our hungry eyes? We were all green with envy. I certainly was, having been deprived of pretty much everything by that immensely rich bastard father of mine, who refused to spend any money on me, not because he was a miser, but because he was cruel and mean-spirited.

So try and get some closure and leave me in peace. Please keep quiet… Please.'

He fell silent.

I asked myself, 'Why is he so tormented? What did his father's own personal tragedy matter in comparison to the assassination of Abbane Ramdane by certain members of the Organisation, and to the murder of Ben Mhidi by the French army and that swine Bigeard? Or compared to the execution of Fernand Yveton, whose executioner – Fernand Meyssonnier, also known as 'Mr Algiers' – said after the deed, 'He was exemplary as a condemned man. And I mean exemplary. Not like the others that shat themselves. Pathetic! My second customer, Ferradj Mohammed, had screamed and spat and put up a struggle at the guillotine. As for Fernand Yveton, now that was classy…' Omar and I often thought about those other martyrs, who'd been overcome with fear when they'd come face to face with that horrible machine. We wanted to know who they were… We admired them more than the Zabanas, the Talebs, the Yvetons. Classy! What the…?

The Ferradj case was very unusual. He'd only joined the resistance after having been a *harki*, when he'd committed atrocities against the local population. One day, he killed a French soldier over a trifle. Afraid of the French army's reprisals, he sought sanctuary with the resistance. Ferradj had no beliefs. That's why he didn't have the courage to face the guillotine. Omar and I didn't like heroes all that much, which is why we had a soft spot for him. Why? Because fear is so human! And there you have it, this country's painful history sticks in my throat – all thanks to Omar, his complaints, his unhappiness, his epic benders, those fucking teenage years when he and I had done something which we never mentioned ever again after he left to join the resistance. That incredible story of the twins... Nymphos? Maybe, but that's precisely why we loved them, because they were free spirits.

It was true that Uncle Kamal had been unjustly branded a collaborator by one of his underlings! It was also true that Uncle Kamal had been very handsome.

1957, the year of that dramatic attack on the Stade de Colombes, had also witnessed the wholesale liquidation of communist elements within the Organisation, among them the group commanded by Master Amrani in the Aurès, which numbered over three hundred (Muslim, Jewish, Christian, atheist) communist fighters. Their throats were slit in the space of a single night. Among the fallen were Professor Cognot, a lung specialist at the hospital in Constantine, and Ahmed Inal, the first Algerian to qualify as a French teacher and also the national 800 metres champion. It's also true that Salim, Omar's younger brother, had enlisted with the OAS, not out of conviction, but so as to get invited to the Saturday night dances. To increase his chances of laying colonial girls. The cunt. In the end, he got what was coming to him. He had truly deserved his death. He had gone on Arab-killing sprees through the centre of Batna armed with a machine gun, parading his racism in full view. He thought he was a tough guy, with his cherub-like looks, the *pied noir* accent he had quickly learnt to parrot, his nice suits, his sports cars and the beautiful women driven wild by sex, champagne and blood. Blood!

Even worse, I later learnt that Salim had been a divisional head of the OAS! He was neither a fanatic nor politically motivated. He wanted women to like him, particularly settlers' daughters. He didn't need to slaughter dozens of Algerians to achieve that! He had his good looks and his father was a Police Commissioner. The European girls were already crazy about him. He'd overdone it. He was assassinated the day after Independence, amid all the celebrations. Where? How? By whom? No one ever knew. Omar spent long months making the necessary enquiries and had come to the conclusion that Salim had either been murdered out of jealousy or by accident. That he'd never belonged to the OAS. That he was innocent. He was distraught at being unable to mourn his brother properly because there was no corpse. He wove a web of paranoia and cocooned himself inside it. He of all people, an officer in the resistance, had failed miserably… Uncle Kamal didn't deserve all the humiliation and dishonour and the widespread opprobrium that ultimately made him lose his mind, and wander, silent and dishevelled, around the very town where he had been the Police Commissioner only a few months earlier.

I was the only person who still listened to Omar. I helped him attain a certain level of clarity. I wanted to relieve him of the guilt he had been mired in since 1 November 1954, the day the war had begun. What a waste of time! It invariably wound up with him getting angry at me and not speaking to me for months, then coming back to apologise, crestfallen and unhappy, suffering from a profound sense of hurt, even though he was now aware of the truth. He was also conscious of how he was deceiving himself and would eventually get back in touch with me. There was a childhood complicity between us. We had spent fantastic summers together on his grandfather's farms and on the beach. There had been the brothels of Constantine. There had been the twins. Above all the twins! Those girls had by now become an unspoken taboo between us, but I was determined sooner or later to break the silence. I bided my time. This trip between Algiers and Constantine would be decisive in that respect as well!

Those unspeakable summers on the Eastern Algerian plateaus, not far from Constantine, at harvest time, when horses were broken in and furious stallions made to copulate, when hectares of wheat fields were strewn with the stark red stains of Barbary figs. Those Barbary figs had been a staple part of our summer holidays, their different shades – ranging from green to brown and red – with that trademark stiffness that made them seem so much more violent to us, so much more real. A raw, rugged quality that brought to mind the paintings of Marcel Gromaire and Fernand Léger… To us, the Barbary figs were symbolic guardians that had always kept watch over our country. Despite all the disasters and the tragedies, despite the genocide!

It was because of this idyllic past – undoubtedly exaggerated by nostalgia and my imagination – that I had remained so jealously affectionate towards Omar, who was after all only a cousin by marriage. He was only a nephew of my aunt, who had married my uncle Hocine, a perverse, obese idiot, whom I hated for his cruelty. The real reason for my friendship with Omar, apart from his tragic destiny, was the fabulous wardrobe whose contents he proudly exhibited each summer. When we were teenagers, he would often lend me his suits so we could go to Azefoun – or Bougie or Bône or Philippeville or Djidjelli or Collo or La Calle – and flirt with the settlers' daughters who organised dances on the beaches.

There were also the twins, and the mad orgies we had with them. And Mozart, my tame hedgehog, who I had taught to whistle Bach sonatas and had incomprehensibly turned into a music-lover. There was Nana, my cat. There were bottles of whisky and wine from Mascara. There were memorable piss-ups and memories of our talented classmates at secondary school. There was the bachelor lifestyle we'd chosen when we were teenagers and that continued to bind us. Why? It was all a pretext for Omar to come and visit me in that house of mine in Constantine, which he'd personally restored so beautifully.

There lay the Gordian knot of our complex, muddled, almost amorous relationship. It was certainly true that he'd gone into the bush and joined the resistance right after second-ary school, going against his father's wishes without a second thought. Two years older than me, Omar had become a hero in my eyes, and at the age of eighteen I followed in his footsteps and enlisted.

There was something else going on between us, a secret of sorts. Something that we had done together when we were teenagers, but never since brought up.

Something strange.

Inappropriate.

A few weeks after I joined the resistance, Omar had sent me a terse little note imbued with irony: 'I hope you haven't got too many blisters and that you're getting on well with the crabs. Welcome to the Aurès.' That was before he sent that photograph.

On the plane the mood was calm. Some people were queuing up for the toilets. I looked at my watch. We had been airborne for twenty minutes.

Omar looked at me distractedly. He was pretending to doze. I knew he was wide-awake. We were each carrying on our con-versation deep down inside us. I adored this man, this cousin of mine, this communist, this piss-head, this architect who had once worked for Oscar Niemeyer, the great Brazilian architect and project manager, who was still alive at the age of 101, and whom Omar admired for his design of Constantine University, a work of genius. Omar went to Rio de Janeiro every year to pay his respects to his idol. He called it his 'Brazilian pilgrimage'.

But I too had had my share of unhappiness. I lost my paternal grandfather when I was a child. He perished in a fire when his grocery store burnt down during the *Mawlid* festivities, a fire started by some kid who'd set off a firecracker for fun. My grandfather lost his life and I lost my child-like tenderness, since I had adored my grandfather and hated my father.

Mohammed, my grandfather, was tiny and light-skinned, with blue eyes and a bushy red moustache. He was incredibly frightened of his wife, who was rather ugly, nagging, malicious and obese, just like her son, Uncle Hocine, who was her favourite, and whom she daily force-fed a variety of snacks and desserts. She found her husband too soft-spoken and gentle, almost effeminate. 'He's fragile,' she would say. This was neither praise nor criticism; it was much worse. It was mockery.

My grandfather bore a striking resemblance to Si Mustafa, Omar's grandfather. They were the same height. Had the same complexion. The same eyes. The same moustache. And the same kindness that sprang from nowhere and which both men freely lavished on others. Despite the class differences between them, they spent a lot of time together, talking, discussing politics, lending each other books. But my grandfather was just a well-off merchant, whereas Omar's grandfather was actually wealthy. He was the one who filled Omar's wardrobes with such wonderful clothes, designer shirts and shoes that were certainly Italian and sometimes even handmade in Milan,

Turin or Venice. I didn't know about that until much later. That is to say until this decisive trip we were taking, during which time we were getting everything off our chests. All in the space of a single hour.

Despite their different backgrounds, the two men got on and respected one another. When my grandfather's son, my uncle Hocine, married Ouarda, Si Mustafa's daughter, there was no question of a dowry. Just a single, symbolic franc! This marriage strengthened their friendship and when my grandfather died in the fire, his friend never quite recovered from the loss. He subconsciously considered me an orphan from that point on, perhaps because he knew how unusually profound a love I had cherished for my grandfather, and Si Mustafa therefore treated me like one of his own grandchildren, a situation I accepted. Every summer, he would insist on inviting me to his stud farms and holiday homes, which were scattered all over eastern Algeria, between Azefoun and Djidjelli, by way of Bône, Bougie and Philippeville.

That was how I became Omar's best friend, thanks to his grandfather.

It was the beginning of a great friendship, which had its fair share of difficulties, arguments, rows and reconciliations, and had a hand in shaping my own destiny, because I in truth modelled my own life on Omar's and imitated each step I took in life on his. To this day I am convinced that I would never have joined the resistance in July 1959 had it not been for him. He'd enlisted two years earlier, leaving the Organisation in France to return to Algeria and become a resistance fighter in Chaabet Lakhra, one of the most remote parts of the Aurès mountains.

Before he left France, Omar was assigned a very difficult mission as a test. They had ordered him to kill a big-shot

Algerian collaborator – the *bashagha* Ali Chekkal, a ruthless, crooked old man – during the French Cup final on 26 May 1957 in which FC Toulouse was playing Angers SCO at the Stade de Colombes. The *bashagha* was seated next to René Coty, the French President.

Omar – who had been saddled with the alias of 'Joe' by the resistance – accepted the mission, but the orders were counter-manded at the last minute, by which point the Organisation had already discussed the plan with him and even given him a ticket for the VIP stand. So he didn't go through with it. They had only wanted to put him to the test; to size up his determination and resolve. He felt terribly let down and it had haunted him ever since. He kept up with the news about the executioner after the latter's arrest. The little plumber. He knew everything about him. When Independence came, Omar was finally able to meet him, and he introduced me to him. After he had killed the *bashagha* and been arrested, this militant, whose name was Mohammed Ben Sadok, had commanded the French policemen's respect.

He had satisfied his pride. His path and destiny resembled that of Fernand Yveton – the difference of course being that Yveton was executed and Mohammed Ben Sadok was par-doned, thanks to the efforts of a committee of French intel-lectuals, as well as a series of public demonstrations of support. Caught red-handed, Ben Sadok had decided that he wouldn't allow his torturers to get away with all their condescending and racist abuse. (At the time, 'fig tree' was the racist slur for Algerians, though for us, Barbary figs were a symbol of resist-ance.) He needed to be calmer than them. Look them in the eye. Pride is a shield. He had history on his side. The Police Commissioner in Colombes wasn't really up to the task, and after numerous failed attempts at prosecution, he progressively lost his arrogance, his cheeky humour and even his broken, suburban French. The plumber had mounted quite a simple defence: he refused to concede even a single inch.

In the disorganised, dusty police station, the balance of power was decidedly uneven, since the terrorist's calm demeanour was clearly nerve-shattering for everyone around him, save for the Commissioner. He was lolling in his worn imitation-leather armchair, his face made even paler by the insufficient light cast by the room's single light bulb. There was also a typist on the other side of the room, who was tasked with writing up the report; he felt every click of the keys shiver down his back as he tried to picture the outdated typewriter which – due to the metallic sound the carriage made each time a letter was printed and the interference the keyboard produced like a stifled cough – just had to be an old Remington.

Behind him stood the policemen, their arms crossed against their Judoka chests, stuck in their usual routine of petty thefts, ridiculous murders, car accidents, handbag thefts, acts of vandalism and all manner of other offences – and here they were, confronted with a headline-grabbing assassination that had shaken the whole of France and demonstrated the Organisation's power. The policemen kept silent when faced with the terrorist's reasoned argument, which he had outlined both calmly and concisely when they asked him to explain his actions. Arguments he repeated monotonously throughout the night without once missing a beat, impressing the policemen to the point where no one dared talk down to him, and making the Commissioner wary of meeting the man's steady, almost contemptuous gaze.

The prisoner was more than ready to sketch out all the steps that had led him to his act in big dark red strokes, painting them a picture of the disaster that involved the execution of a traitor (the reason he had been specifically targeted), and a reconstruction of the whole trajectory that took many secondary details into account: the whole gamut and constellation of gestures and movements and the layout of the public places he had walked through, where he had left fingerprints and the weapon he had used, as well as a whole arsenal of minute details which he did not really care to remember, but outlined regardless.

The policemen stood still, their eyelids already blue with rising tension and astonishment they were trying to rein in — to say nothing of the panic that was throbbing in their nerves and temples. They could not believe their eyes: they were faced with a real political bombshell. They were frightened by the culprit's audacity and the calm with which he had fired his bullet, without even taking the gun out of his pocket, without even taking his aim, almost randomly, because the *bashagha* had walked straight into him as he was being escorted out of the stadium for security reasons, well before the end of the match.

FC TOULOUSE: 6
SCO ANGERS: 3

He had fired his miniature revolver almost casually through the cloth of his China-blue jacket and hit the bull's eye from a distance of thirteen yards. The policemen were suddenly thrust onto the stage of history when they had just been getting ready to go home and have a quiet dinner with the family and settle down to watch the latest detective thriller on television.

Stunned by the magnitude of the event that had just occurred, they had lost all concept of time, forgetting to call their wives and girlfriends to warn them that they wouldn't be coming home that night.

He, on the other hand, gathered his thoughts and set about eliminating this sterile profusion of details and incidents that seemed to fascinate the policemen so much. He was staring so fixedly at the space in front of him that he felt dizzy. He wasn't thinking about anything, not even of Messaouda, his mother, who would certainly refuse to attend the trial. He was relieved that so many of the streets, cities and continents he had travelled through would now be devoted to the Organisation, thanks in part to the success of his mission. He was amazingly steadfast in refusing to be misled by the policemen's ambiguous questions: What does this postcard mean with the picture of an Etruscan statuette on it, this champions' trophy with winged feet, these blueprints of refineries in Rouen, Le Havre and Mourepiane (later the targets of dramatic attacks)?

He limited himself to repeating the same, clear arguments, telling them that they were wasting their time, that they had only to open his wallet and pull out that cherished blue postcard, whose gelatinous film was likely to flake off in the policemen's big hairy hands, almost angry at the attention they paid to the card and their attempts to establish some link with the blueprint of the refinery in Rouen. 'They're so dim-witted and clumsy', he thought to himself, laughing at how they held the postcard and examined it as if it concealed some indecipherable hieroglyphs, all the more so since – as he would later find out – the Etruscans had a written language that hadn't yet been decoded, as if it were booby-trapped, as if it were magical.

He had an irrepressible desire to sleep and gather his

thoughts, leaving the policemen to their far-fetched assumptions, their illogical reasoning, their idle chatter, their futile arguments and the limits of their little brains, which had grown used to their petty routine, their small-time delinquents and all the small, trivial affairs of a suburban police station.

As it happens, the police chief never stopped phoning his officers up to remind them that he wanted to know all the details, ramifications, names of accomplices, the plans, the sort of organisation, its command structure, its support mechanisms, the places of rendezvous, the names of the big leaders as well as those of simple underlings, the weapons caches, the contacts, their supply sources, the location of clandestine printing presses and of hide-outs, and information on some of their French accomplices and the Organisation's sympathisers, who were considered a bunch of criminals. He demanded to know their names, their addresses, and the secret codes the members of this network used to communicate with one another. He wanted the man who had murdered the *bashagha* to furnish them with all imaginable, possible details, but he didn't want them to lay a finger on him, let alone torture or humiliate him. He demanded a full and detailed report, complete with forecast statistics, homothetic curves, probability studies, solid hypotheses and robust conclusions.

The Police Commissioner was shouting down the telephone, saying he didn't want to hear of any blunders, excessive zeal or errors, because, he yelled, the whole world would hear about it – as would journalists from every country, because this business was serious enough as it was and he didn't want it to blow up in his face, because, you never know, with these abrupt sea-changes in politics – all the more so since there was a ministerial crisis going on at the moment – he didn't want someone to make him take the fall. 'After all, I am the one who has to deal with all the hearings, the rogatory commissions, the loud-mouth newspapers, the solidarity meetings, the motions signed by those bloody intellectuals, the popular demonstrations, the hunger strikes, all the jeering at the UN, the interventions by the International Red Cross and Red Crescent committees, and so on.'

A FRIEND OF FRANCE, THE
BASHAGHA ALI CHEKKAL, KILLED
AT THE STADE DE COLOMBES DURING
THE FRENCH CUP FINAL
FC TOULOUSE: 6
SCO ANGERS: 3

'I know the score, boys,' said the old Commissioner. 'You're going to do a good job for me within the seven days of custody. A week flies by. You better believe it! After that the prisoner will be transferred to the custody of the prosecutor and we can't rely on the judge assigned to the case, because a whole plethora of lawyers have offered their services to the man. So get a move on! But restrain yourselves. I want him in one piece. A word of advice: pay close attention to the subway map, the blueprints of the refinery in Rouen, the reproduction of the Etruscan or Thracian or Byzantine or whatever fucking civilization that statuette belongs to… And find me that 'Joe' who was in touch with him…'

At the end of the war, Omar and I asked ourselves just how it was that the same Organisation that had brought the French army to its knees, and had had the audacity and the means to take the war home to the French, could then go on to commit such terrible crimes. The three hundred villagers slaughtered at Mellouza. And the murder of Abbane Ramdane, who had been strangled by one of the most respected leaders of the resistance with the complicity of Krim Belkacem, who had hidden in the adjacent room during the deed like a coward. Belkacem was no doubt convinced he was doing the right thing. Saving the revolution. But the irony of history is that he himself was later strangled in a hotel room in Frankfurt a few years after Independence! Because history never forgets. It only seems to. Then there was the murder of Master Amrani's Muslim, Christian and Jewish communist group in the Aurès (two or three hundred of them) – formidable fighters who had had their throats slit in a single night with the Organisation's tacit approval. And many more... There had been so many fratricidal wars, so much frightening settling of scores. How had that come to pass? Why? This war: this cancer!

The Algerian terrorist continued to maintain that he'd had no contact with the Organisation, that he was altogether incapable of taking part in a group or movement since he was – as he mischievously admitted – too much of an individualist. He didn't want to get Messaouda, his mother, mixed up in this business, which was why he hadn't thought it worthwhile to tell them about the postcard, even though he had bought it with the intention of sending it to her to mark this important day; he had later changed his mind on the off-chance the athlete's penis might have offended his mother's sensibilities.

Moreover, hadn't Pleimelding, despite being Toulouse Football Club's centre-back and captain, told journalists and the radio before the match in the changing rooms filled with the musky sweat of the athletes' bodies – already overheated by the cries of the roaring crowd as well as the stage fright they felt due to the importance of this final of the French Cup – hadn't Pleimelding spontaneously announced that he would do everything he could to win the Cup so he could present it to his mother – who had stayed behind in her village in Alsace – as a Mother's Day gift on the 31st, a few days after the match?

Omar was already in the bush by then and was able to follow all the events as they unfolded on his transistor radio: the trial, the death sentence and the pardon he received thanks to the help of the watchful guardians of France's real conscience at the time, led by Jean-Paul Sartre and Simone de Beauvoir.

Omar knew that the Organisation had decided around the same time to evacuate every professional Algerian footballer to Tunisia, where they then grew into the formidable team that would wreak havoc in stadiums all over the world and bring untold prestige to the resistance. Omar often spoke to me about the assassination attempt he was due to carry out... It haunted him. So did the Algerian footballers' escape.

The escape of the 32 footballers, including several members of the French national team such as Zitouni, Mekhloufi and Brahimi, had only been made possible by the assistance of those French men and women who were opposed to this dirty war. And there were many of them. They never stopped organising demonstrations in favour of Algerian Independence. They often lay down in the path of trains transporting conscripts to Algeria. There had been the Charonne station massacre of January 1962, whose victims had been French communists opposed to the war in Algeria.

There had been the horrifying racist attacks on Algerians on 17 October 1961 in Paris. We talked about them all the time and thought about our hero and teacher, Mr Baudier. When James Dean died, he had told us to our saddened faces, 'He has bought himself a luxury death in a car that cost more than the average American worker earns in a lifetime! There you go boys… Now stop whining!' When we chanced upon some isolated French soldiers in the bush, we left them alone, telling ourselves that at least a few of them must sympathise with our cause and must have been drafted against their will. We therefore avoided catching them in our ambushes and hid this from our unrelenting commanders.

Later, after Independence, when we were at university, Omar much admired the Colombes terrorist, Mohammed Ben Sadok. He had become friends with him. I was both exasperated and jealous.

The plane continued on its way.

Chapter IX

THE ORGANISATION was both thorough and demanding, but it was made up of human beings who were as capable of bravery, honesty and conscientiousness as they were of being cowardly, spineless, petty and selfish. Omar had drummed this sort of talk into me since the year of Independence, when we graduated and broke off from the Organisation. When he started harping on like that, I knew he would invariably end up talking about Boussouf's assassination of Abbane Ramdane – ordered by Krim Belkacem and other high-ranking leaders in the Organisation – as well as Bigeard's murder of Ben Mhidi. The two men's destinies were so similar that we were fascinated by the coincidences. Both were uncompromising intellectuals and the real brains and strategists behind the war effort. Both were killed on isolated farmsteads, one near Tétouan, the other close to Algiers.

Abbane Ramdane had been put to death in Tétouan by his own brothers-in-arms. Ben Mhidi was executed by Bigeard, who went around claiming that he had been his friend. This duplicity made us beside ourselves with anger. The two murders worried us, all the more so since Ben Mhidi's French executioner had staged his suicide: he had had to hang him three times because the rope kept breaking! Yet victory was meagre and small.

We often spoke of how Independence had turned sour, of widespread corruption and tribal bickering. We therefore posed ourselves this inevitable question: How had the Organisation, which had comported itself so impeccably throughout the seven-year war, turned into such a dishonest, money-grubbing, arrogant and finally idiotic government?

From the first days of Independence, the factions in the Organisation had started fighting amongst themselves with a violence, savagery and furious determination that had distressed Omar and I. After a few days of public jubilation, the Kasbah in Algiers – the Organisation's stronghold during the seven long years of the war – became the focal point of bloody clashes between rival groups. The crowd refused to accept such fratricidal madness and kept shouting a single, simple slogan: 'Seven years is enough!'

Every day we took part in the angry, unarmed crowds that denounced this civil war. As if seven years of war, a year of looting, and organised carnage by the OAS in the country's main cities hadn't sufficed. We still had to go through this Kasbah war, which in fact ushered in a cycle of violence that has yet to end.

During the month of July 1962, I was almost killed by a gang leader who had decreed that I was an undercover French agent because I was blond. Omar stood by, completely helpless. The crowd wanted to come to my aid and tear me from the clutches of the armed men, but they didn't manage to.

Suddenly, an old woman wearing a veil confronted the leader of the group and asserted that there was something Algerian about me, regardless of the colour of my skin and my hair. The thug was taken aback by the old woman's comments, and the crowd took advantage of the distraction to grab hold of me and free me from the claws of those new predators that were taking the country hostage.

I was saved from certain death that day. Omar often spoke to me about that terrible episode. I trembled each time he brought it up. A panic-like fear took hold of me. I started dripping with sweat. Shivering with cold.

As I do to this day.

That same year, after the attempt on my life, Omar and I decided to join the Communist Party. Our shared political allegiances also played an important role in our relationship. The Organisation was no longer effective and had lost all credibility. In the first years of the war, several cracks had started to show: the struggle for power and the lust for money were now all they stood for.

Abbane Ramdane and Ben Mhidi had been the first to sense this disaster. They were the only intellectuals in the high command. Paradoxically, they were both killed in the same year, 1957, one by the Algerians, the other by the French. When we discussed these men's deaths, Omar and I were fascinated by this conveniently-timed historical concurrence, as well as the propensity of history to juxtapose subjectivity with the objectivity of real life. I was pleased with Omar's obsession with this particular theory, as well as his overall fascination with history. We were very much in agreement on this point. But as soon as he began to analyse his family's case, he lost all his good humour and plunged headfirst into paranoia. And, knowing he was wrong, he would quickly change the subject and return to the assassination of Abbane Ramdane and Ben Mhidi: it was easier. He knew how to be a coward when it suited him.

He would tell me then, to commandeer the conversation: 'They were both killed in the same circumstances. Abbane Ramdane in a farm near Tétouan in Morocco where a few chiefs of the Organisation had set a trap for him, and Ben Mhidi also on a farm close to Algiers where Bigeard gave a one-eyed intelligence officer the order to hang him. They were both 'amicably' executed... Can you believe it... In a bare room in an isolated farmhouse near Tétouan. The one with a rope slipped around his neck from behind. And a bare room in a farm close to Algiers. The other with a noose around his neck. That is the definition of solitude...'

I said, 'History is something ridiculous, or rather it's crammed full of ridicule... Do you know that Abbane's murderer praised him to high heaven before executing him? Do you know that Bigeard paid tribute to Ben Mhidi before having him hanged? I know that you know all about this down to the smallest detail, but I have always found this so utterly crazy, despite how dramatic it was... History, what a bitch! And a cynic to boot.'

He said, 'And that terrifying farce that Bigeard's goon – that one-eyed Aussaresses – played on him: after having hanged his victim and determined he was dead, he took him to the hospital, to A&E or intensive care. How do I know? The madness! The worst things often come from the top of the hierarchy, turning history into a panic-stricken dog who no longer knows which way it's going...'

Ben Mhidi was secretly hanged by the French army on 11 February 1957 at a farm near Douera, twenty miles from Algiers. Maurice Audin, a young and brilliant professor of mathematics at the University of Algiers and a fellow traveller, was arrested on 21 June 1957, then tortured and murdered by Bigeard's paratroopers, who buried him in a hole, the location of which remains unknown to this day. Fernand Yveton, also a fellow traveller, and what is more a *pied noir*, was guillotined on 11 February 1957 by his French executioners in Algiers's Barbarossa prison. The same day Ben Mhidi was executed! Yveton's executioner, a jolly, roly-poly man called Fernand Meyssonnier, who was known as Mr Algiers, declared after the execution: 'He was an exemplary prisoner!' The executioner and his victim had the same first name – yet another coincidence for Omar and I, who loved this accumulation of futile details that are the stuff history is made of.

History, that terrible maelstrom.

Many days after we had discussed all these assassinations, executions, treacherous statements, secret words, enigmatic smiles and macabre shows, Omar phoned me from Constantine to talk about everything and nothing: about a new project he was about to start, the restoration of the city's hanging bridge, similar work being done on Ahmed Bey's palace, and even of how pleasant the weather was and about the heavy snow that had fallen on the city in the past few days. Then, as he was about to hang up, he suddenly said, 'You're right – I'm wrong to focus on my father and brother. There was much worse, there was Abbane Ramdane, Ben Mhidi, Yveton, Maillot, Audin and the millions of civilian victims.' He fell silent for a few seconds and then added, 'And this revolution, which betrayed itself from the very beginning.'

I said to myself, 'Indeed. This revolution that betrayed us!'

The passengers were getting restless. They were looking out of their windows at the foothills around Constantine, a city that was 2,000 years old and was known as Cirta in Roman times.

The colonial wars had never actually come to an end. War, this carnival to which foolish soldiers traipsed off and always lost, trudging through the muddy Vietnamese marshes, catching all sorts of diseases like foot-and-mouth, or yellow fever, dying as they cried out for their mothers, their mouths full of mosquitoes, their flocculent bodies slowly decomposing; deteriorating rapidly as the tropical climate is quicker than any ambulance, any rescue helicopter, any combat fighter, any chemical or nuclear weapon... Bubbling with heat, the slimy, marshy vapours and that unbelievable sweat trickling from God knows where: the body seemed to be capable of pumping it up and out again at a frightening pace.

These stupid, perennial losers of the colonial wars, yomping through the icy Algerian winters and the mossy Vietnamese jungle, contracting all types of hepatitis, dying as they cried out for their fathers, their mouths full of ants, their frozen bodies washed away by the mad, raging streams flooding down from the Atlas mountains, bodies later found torn to shreds in oases like Mchounèche, Tolga and Timimoun, where the first heat waves of the Saharan spring stripped them to the bone in the blink of an eye, helped by voracious horned vipers and the countless ants...

Before dying, these men had often been in the hands of torturers brimming with courage and arrogance because they worked in groups of a dozen while they tortured, clobbered, electro-shocked and humiliated, savagely inflicting all manner of imaginable pain on a single, unarmed human being as he lay there naked and de-humanised; not because there were single standards, but because deep down the tortured man chuckled to himself about the absurdities of this so-called logic that connected all these injustices.

Injustices that Omar and I had fiercely condemned since our teenage years. Zygote, my twin brother, who was three minutes younger than me, never took part in our debates on the colonial horrors. He poked fun at us: 'Like fuck you're going to kick the French out!'

Of all these horrors, I retained only a single image, which has haunted me throughout my life – that of a little nomad boy running out of his tent and heading towards a French soldier who was pointing a pistol at him. The child ran all the faster because he thought it was a toy. Then the soldier fired. The child falling. Then everything went black. A black hole. That split second, encapsulating the whole of human barbarism, marked me for life.

My whole life I have been stuck in that footage shot by the French army's news service because it was then that I understood that objects could transcend their utilitarian purpose to become the instruments of a very different type of upheaval, one that was altogether more meaningful and explicit and symbolically charged with an infinite number of readings, more than a single human brain – even that of a perverse genius – is capable of imagining, understanding, developing or – what's the slang word for it? – 'swotting up on', maybe!

A bullet smashing a four-year-old's brain! My world turned upside down that day.

'There must be a ruthless clampdown, France reaches from Flanders to the Congo!' One of their ministers repeated this mantra every time he visited Algeria. A minister of something or other, like the Home Secretary or the Minister of Justice, or any of those other terms I have heard since I was a child; a minister of something or other, or the President of the Republic or something else, something similar, something stuffy, plastic, slick, pout-lipped.

Following the example of all those heads of state, those

kings, monarchs, despots and dictators who set themselves up in power for life, or near enough. These unshakeable, deceptively calm, nigh-on mummified men, quietly laughing about geriatric heads of state younger than them, who are just as stuffy, plastic and slick, not to mention odious; men who actually believe that not only the world, but the whole of humanity would fall apart were it not for their efforts; that their absence would unleash the final and definitive apocalypse, the chaos of cosmic proportions so often predicted, emphasised and exaggerated in all the revealed books. It was precisely to Orléansville, one year after the city had been hit by an earthquake in September 1954, that he (the minister) had come to spout his insanities, and I remember remarking on his formal, slightly insidious manner, with that plastic, mummified, slick air about him – with that powdered-up, figurehead skull of his! – a little half-witted, a little nasty. This newspaper headline rang in my ears throughout my childhood and adolescence.

THERE MUST BE A RUTHLESS CLAMPDOWN, GENTLEMEN! FRANCE REACHES FROM FLANDERS TO THE CONGO!

It was somewhat hypocritical therefore that at the height of his power and glory – for he was the President of the Republic, was he not? – he had had the simultaneously daft and nauseating nerve to declaim that he was only concerned with human rights, the rights of minorities and all sorts of other hypocritical nonsense, which he had never for a single moment believed in throughout his long and evil career as a wily and inimitable politician.

On the other hand, the tragic destiny of the other man – the communist, terrorist, *pied noir* and traitor – had profoundly disturbed me. And my mother too.

THE EUROPEAN PUBLIC SEES THE EXECUTION OF THE COMMUNIST TERRORIST AS THE ULTIMATE PROOF OF FRANCE'S DETERMINATION TO PUNISH THE TERRORISTS

He had expected a stay of execution because he was innocent, because he had never killed anyone, because the small bomb he was supposed to place under an old, broken-down, abandoned truck to cause a commotion, as a form of protest, had never left his locker. Something that enlightened, smartly-dressed man – who was caked in make-up each time he appeared on television – was well aware of, since at the time he was, as they were so fond of pompously saying, Minister of Justice! Keeper of the Seals indeed! There was something about this expression which seemed to hint at mouldy little secrets, of conspiracies muffled by thick carpets and sound-proof doors, of base, cowardly actions whose essential secret and fundamental axis, the deepest origins of this chronic, innate, congenital disease, was the lust for power. The very same power that had made him dispatch numerous Algerian patriots of various denominations to the guillotine. 'This symbol of civilisation arrived in Algiers and stood before the astonished eyes of a large number of women, men, Arabs, Jews and Europeans who had rushed to gather around the steamboat that had brought him from France,' Victor Hugo had gibed in 1842. The guillotine had also been the fate of that simple metal worker Yveton. At the time, my mother had asked me, 'Is it true that the eyes continue to move around after the head has tumbled into the basket below? Is it true? But that's horrible, that's frightening – especially considering he hasn't done anything wrong and he's innocent.' And Zygote, ever cruel, told her as a joke: 'Of course they do, Mother. Their eyes continue to move about and their hair and fingernails continue to grow! But what's that got to do with you? After all, he's nothing but a fucking infidel and a communist! Good riddance!'

Initially, when Fernand Yveton was arrested, she had been indifferent to his fate because he was a European and a communist, and it took me two months to get her to reconsider, to change her mind, to take an interest in the fate of the condemned man – a tactic that was so successful that she began to have terrible nightmares about it and became obsessed with Yveton, buying all the newspapers and cutting out every article and snippet that mentioned his case, showing a terribly passionate interest in the trial. Not that it was anything more than a semblance of a trial, a botched and hurried affair where all the decisions had been rushed through in ten days of proceedings. Arrested on 14 November 1956, Yveton was sentenced to death on 24 November 1956. Because he had been caught in flagrante... What was it now? How did they put it? *In flagrante delicto*! Ten days for the pre-trial investigation (including cross-examination and torture) and one day for the trial!

Mother, who had been distraught ever since the verdict, no longer slept and would wake up in the middle of the night to come to my room and ask me lots of questions, demanding that I give her a crash course in politics, proffer psychological explanations and details, always more details about the condemned man. She prevented me from sleeping (well actually, from plunging back into my own nightmares): always talking, so as not to find herself alone in her room, where she would begin to feel frightened, seeing shadows lurking everywhere around her and hearing voices, whispers, moaning, weeping and remonstrations. It got to the point where I would phone Omar for help in the middle of the night, since on some days I could no longer put up with this madness that had begun to wreak havoc on mother's mind, nor could I put up any longer with my monozygotic twin brother Zygote's pathological, aggravating cynicism. (We had nicknamed my brother 'Zygote' around the age of seven or eight, because he was my monozygotic twin. Omar and I hated him because he was so cruel, perverse and treacherous.)

My mother had become an anxious, anorexic wreck. She suggested cooking a few dishes that I might take to the condemned man on death row, regardless of the fact that the prisoner wasn't allowed to accept anything of the sort, nor even clothes or a blanket; only a little money that Béa, his wife, would send via a secure money order that took weeks to reach him, and even this could not exceed the sum of 5,000 francs and could only be sent once a month. And Yveton – who knows why – kept his accounts in order, putting his little CTD (Condemned To Death) nest egg to one side, wearing old, coarse clothes cut from worn-out blankets. His trousers were painted around the buttocks with red acrylic paint that glowed in the dark in case the prisoner escaped – as if an escaped death-row convict on the run wouldn't take his trousers off and run naked into the distance if need be, not only to save his buttocks, but to save his skin. So Fernand Yveton kept his accounts in a little squared notebook.

INCOME on 20/11/56: 1,878 francs;
on 10/12/56: 5,000 francs. Total 6,878 francs.
EXPENSES on 30/11/56: 1,105 francs,
on 02/12/56: 517 francs; on 09/12/56: 1,903 francs.
Total: 3,525 francs.
BALANCE: 6,878 − 3,525 = 3,353 francs.

Perhaps he did this to prove to Béa that he didn't need any money, that there was no need for her to send any, knowing she was living in abject poverty and eking out a miserable living by working as a seamstress, a position from which she was soon dismissed. Or maybe he just did it to pass the time, a little like his copying out popular, soppy romantic songs like *Moulin Rouge*, *I Have Seen In Your Eyes*, *Two Little Shoes* and *Flamenco of Love* into that same squared notebook, regardless of the fact that he already knew them by heart.

Anxious, depressed, anorexic and unable to sleep, Mother wanted to make a few dishes for Yveton, evidently unaware of all the laws, customs and habits that regulated life in those gloomy prisons. She no longer had any doubt that he would be pardoned by the then Minister of Justice, who was still alive and more powerful than ever – just as much of a wheeler-dealer, just as crafty and astute – a man who made it look as if he had been born with a humanist halo around his head. Neither did my mother doubt she would one day meet Yveton, and she even went so far as to suggest that we should invite his wife, Béa, over to the house. I would make fun of her at this point, horsing around, saying, 'Because she's almost got the same name as you – Béia, Béa. Just one letter off, Mother, but you pronounce them almost identically!' but I never dared tell her that her sudden interest in politics, in the resistance, in the struggle, in this terrible war that was unfolding in such a merciless, erratic, unjust manner, and, above all, her interest in this infidel, this miscreant, this communist, this *gaouri* was almost certainly due to her metaphysical belief in innocence, which she had acquired since her husband had accused her of adultery.

She didn't even know that adultery existed. Didn't even know what the word meant and, right up to the day she died some thirty years later, never understood what an adulterer was, the word itself being such a vague, peculiar and whimsical concept, something invented by men to pester their poor wives, who, like her, were resigned to their lot.

My mother had become passionate about the fate of a communist of European origin, who was sentenced to death ten days after his arrest and executed two months later. A passion she shared for all the other rebels that were sentenced to death: 400 patriots were guillotined during the seven years of war, one of the first victims being Mohammed Ferradj, who was blind and disabled. Ferradj was executed in May 1956 at the Barbarossa prison in Algiers. That execution had coincided with my father levelling loathsome accusations against my mother – he who had never stopped marrying one woman after the other, then repudiating and divorcing them, going from one mistress to another, capable of carrying on several liaisons at one time, falling madly in love, writing letters, entreating the women who resisted him until they relented, at which point he would then quickly get rid of them, just like that. As if these false accusations of adultery against my mother weren't enough, my father had married Henriette Gozlan, a talented Jewish dressmaker, and, going against his previous practice, hadn't insisted on her converting to Islam as custom demanded. He had made her his concubine, but strangely acknowledged the two children he'd had by her. 'What a bastard!' Omar had said. 'He really is a racist!' It hadn't therefore been possible to bury Henriette in a Muslim cemetery, and she was instead interred in a Jewish one. I had no objections, but Omar did! He spent a number of days running about trying to obtain some false documents certifying that Henriette Gozlan had converted to Islam and married my father in 1948. I didn't understand Omar's attitude. 'What's the difference between a Muslim and a Jewish cemetery?' Omar never did give me an answer.

My bastard of a father continued to travel from continent to continent, securing a string of business deals and sending his famous postcards. His was an insatiable sort of journey, a geography of dissatisfaction, since whenever he went abroad on his trips he didn't just handle money, seal business deals and play the stock exchange; he would also explore women's genitals, their pleats and folds, their flesh and their mouths as if searching for his own despair.

While I was a general practitioner at the Mustafa hospital in Algiers, many years after Independence, in October 1988, at the time of the riots that had laid waste to Algeria, I asked myself what could drive a man to murder, or rather what might have driven those young men – during the terrible riots in October 1988 – to lie in ambush behind a succession of streets the tanks couldn't enter and then kill four or five of their crew? They had shadowed them for days, never leaving their posts, taking turns to keep watch in groups of two or three, working in rotation, staying together, calm despite the untimely assaults, making somewhat comical attempts to gain ground at dizzying speed. One of the boys – the fastest, most athletic and acrobatic amongst them – would run right in front of the tanks and act like a clown and then dash back, his heart falling down to the heels of the Adidas trainers he'd stolen the day before from a gargantuan underground warehouse containing hundreds of thousands of the things, despite the fact that, thanks to the maddening shortages, supplies were now so scarce that the young – and even the old – were positively obsessed with them.

I asked myself what could drive these young boys to be so patient, to endure such hunger, thirst, scorching days and freezing nights, so determined were they to kill those men sitting in their tanks, to slip in right under their noses and lure them out of their vehicles for a second. This achieved, the boys would fall upon them, disarm them, force them to take refuge under their tanks and then toss them a tiny bottle with a little petrol inside and an Adidas shoelace sticking out as a wick to blow them sky-high.

Which means that they blew the tanks up while the soldiers were underneath them, having had the time, all the same, to beg their captors to spare them, to weep, to scream and shout – right up to the moment when the series of blasts rang out, almost simultaneously with an explosion of joy from these youths, who were the same age as those macerated soldiers who had been blown to bits and gone up in smoke. A few days previously these soldiers had been strutting around boasting, even going so far as to imagine that barely pubescent girls crazy with desire were eyeing them through the windows.

The rebels that had blown up the tanks had meanwhile jumped in behind the wheel of the vehicles that had not been damaged and, despite their extreme fatigue and their filthy appearance, they bared their faces and torsos, their flesh and muscles exuding a certain ruthlessness and violence, as well as physical well-being.

These men were in fact little more than children, wet behind the ears, abandoned from an early age, cut off from all tenderness, betrayed by those old rebels who had become the worst sort of exploiters. Arrogant and ignorant, they were harassed on a daily basis by the police and the government, humiliated by the wealth being openly flaunted by a new class of nouveaux riches in love with themselves, behind the wheels of their brand-new cars, some of them even bulletproof, with metallic finishes, air-conditioning and extravagant stereos.

Once their euphoria had faded, their madness had subsided and their hatred had been sated, the rebels stood there without a single word or gesture, watching the illegible traces of the disasters they had left in their wake: an abstract image made even more unreal by the two or three tanks that were still burning, by the two or three undamaged tanks they had climbed into, and by the five or six bodies of the tank crew members that had burnt to cinders in a matter of seconds. The vehicles just kept on burning, as though they had all the time in the world, as if all they had ever aspired to be was a mess of steel and twisted caterpillar tracks.

Omar kept phoning me throughout these events. 'Do you realise! Their tanks are shooting at unarmed kids! Do you realise! We didn't fight to kick the French out for this!' I calmed him down by replying, 'Yes, that isn't why we had to kick the French out, but don't wind yourself up. All revolutions are doomed to failure: this is history in all its complexity. For now, the important thing is to put those bastards that are out shooting at kids where they can do no harm!'

The plane seemed at a standstill despite flying at a speed of five hundred miles an hour...

Chapter X

WHEN I GOT HOME in the evening after a tiring day at the hospital, I had a shower, grabbed a beer and sat down to relax in the garden overlooking the bay of Algiers, whose beauty I never tired of admiring. Outside, the riots had reached their peak.

I had avoided walking along the seafront, my usual route home from work, where I had often strolled with Omar back when both of us were students. The seafront had become unrecognisable. Devastated.

Until the riots, this seafront had been one of the protected areas of the city that had been spared from the clutches of the nouveaux riches, who had disfigured Algiers through the anarchic construction of unbelievably ugly buildings. Exactly why this seafront had escaped their ferocity and voraciousness eluded me. Omar and I asked ourselves this question, but could not come up with any answers.

Situated in the heart of the city, the seafront had always aroused my senses and filled my head with images that Marquet – the French painter who had spent 20 years of his life in this city – had captured so well. This part of Algiers still had a remarkably authentic urban feel to it.

Back there, to the south: the heights of the city climbing up towards the sky. Ahead, to the north: the sea and the docks. On one side lay the neo-Moorish and neo-colonial buildings, visually striking as well as elegant and refined, which, as Omar never stopped repeating while we were at university, were the only wonderful legacy the French had left us! On the other side were the gigantic, inescapable docks, bedecked with complex, interlinked machines which increasingly invaded the urban fabric, devouring it and swallowing it up: they could be seen from all over town. Looming up everywhere. Just there!

When night fell, the seafront looked sublime, its opacity blurring shapes and painting them with a sort of chromatic glimmer, giving strollers the impression that everything was cloaked in exaggerated lethargy, especially the dozens of ships moored along the quay. The impression, that is, that the docks were taking over the city, pressing against it, spilling into it despite its perfectly straight streets, the interminable avenues, its sickly neon lights and the futuristic buildings that still had an air of subterfuge about them, like a film set.

After nightfall, the docks impregnated the city with their unwholesome stench, forcing life in the Kasbah uphill. Towards God, through the alleyways and embellished labyrinths, where unique miniature mosques were to be found scattered here and there!

In that peculiar month of October 1988, the birds had gathered on three or four trees in the garden, as if disdaining the other, less leafy trees. The mulberry tree stood out and the lushness of its layered, dark green obscurity created strangely frightening and funereal shapes. All the objects in the vicinity seemed like ghosts, one piled atop the other at quite close quarters, and tiredness made me feel they were surrounding me like the big, heavy, angry tanks that were roaming around the city. These tanks were settled in comfortably for the long haul, soiling everything with chaos, laying waste and challenging everything including the abnormal weather that was proving disorientating to the soldiers, the demonstrators, my cat Nana and Mozart, my music-loving hedgehog (I schlepped them along with me on my travels between Algiers and Constantine, which is why all my friends and colleagues thought me a little eccentric. Zygote, for his part, used to say that it was high time they locked me up in an asylum. Only Omar found my attitude towards my little menagerie charming and sweet.)

Once, on my way back from the hospital, I sensed the birds growing restless, or rather, jittery in a manner that was unusual for them. Unless these feelings were emanating from me, simply because I was both exhausted and overwhelmed with man's capacity to show such cruelty (especially the manner in which they had castrated Ali, known as 'Nightmare Face', by sticking his penis into a desk drawer and then opening and shutting the drawer methodically, meticulously and bureaucratically, laughing amongst themselves, calling this technique 'the art of tidying one's stuff away properly…').

Mozart the hedgehog was as sensitive as I was to all that muffled late-afternoon orchestration. Nana, on the other hand, was wholly indifferent to it. I was fascinated by this Siamese cat's sense of propriety. At night she slept at the foot of my bed, but when I had a girlfriend stay over, she would spend the night outside! Out of modesty? Out of jealousy? My flights of fancy amused Omar, but as soon as I touched on the subject of our bachelorhood, our inability to get married and have children – in short to be like everyone else – he shut up.

Under my eyelids, which had grown heavy due to the lack of sleep, I felt colours change into their opposites, shifting and alternating. They formed a rectangle, a dark green window separated into two parts: a cherry-red rectangle – my swollen eyelids – and an olive-green rectangle – the lush mulberry tree. Suddenly, I pricked up my ears to their voices, fleeting to start with, but soon swelling. I had a hunch, though sleep had already begun to take a hold of my mind, that an imperceptible change had taken place; despite the fact that – when all was said and done – the air was still the same. It was just the transition from the end of the day to the beginning of night.

The birds began to answer each other hesitantly and intermittently at a barely-audible frequency, as though they were having second thoughts and stuttering, then swiftly taking heart until their perfectly pitched songs rose up from deep inside the mulberry tree and then from every tree in the garden. But the clearest harmonies of all came from the giant mulberry tree, whose branches continued to claw at my bedroom windows. The melody's crescendo was soft and sweet and silky, and was promptly followed by a genuine, swelling concerto full of improvisation. The initial concerto gradually turned into a symphony, sometimes dissonant, sometimes harmonious, occasionally extremely precise.

Then the musical and spatial arrangements began to change – drastically – at extraordinary speed. In one direction the horizon was stained by a greenish streak, and in the other the musical tumult reached its deafening climax. It was as if the old world, struggling and unravelling in its slow, difficult march, acquired a new lease of life, reinvigorated by this symphony of birds that sounded as if it were being performed on old instruments grown rusty with the evening dew. When I raised my eyes – by which time night had been scattered over the garden – I saw groups of birds on the lookout from the roof corners, facing east, their bodies casting blurry, slightly faded little shadows above the uncertain rim of the sky that hadn't yet reverted to its usual shade of blue-black, but was hanging on to wan, faded colours.

Like the sky I'd glimpsed in the badly-reproduced photographs in my jealously hoarded newspapers with their accounts of the terrible earthquake of 1953 (which, in retrospect, seemed like a prelude to the real earthquake that was to come a year later on 1 November 1954, the date that signalled the beginning of the war) that contrasted with the thousands of dappled grey feathers here and there, the millions of round, green leaves looming large, hanging over almost the entire roof of the house and some of the neighbouring houses' roofs, not to mention a good portion of the rest of the sky. I realised then that some residual darkness that had been left hanging during the sunset now seemed to be dripping down with the slowness of stretching quicksilver, or like the dregs of flowing wine.

This in turn drained the habitual greyness from the feathers of the birds lined up along the roof of the house and on the branches of the trees and in the depths of the mulberry tree. Perched on their little legs, the birds had now fallen silent, while slight vibrations occasionally ruffled their puffed-out plumage; the sort of quick vibration that was barely perceptible to the naked eye, matching every trill and every cry, in perfect harmony with this rhythmic music and its ascending, progressively swelling tones, escalating to the point where it became ear-splittingly shrill. It was at this moment that the birds' eyes, though small, seemed clear and gleaming in contrast to their slightly orangey, rosy beaks.

This spectacle, helped by the breeze, gave me some respite. I felt better rested. Little by little, the tiredness I had accumulated during those long days at the hospital began to recede. A sort of serenity took hold of my mind and body, even though I was fully aware that the riots outside were rising towards their inevitable climax.

I was alone, drinking a beer in my garden in Algiers, pricking my ears up at the intermittent sound of explosions going off in the distance. I wondered why I needed such solitude. Why I desired and accepted this bachelorhood, which surprised even me some days.

And why was Omar also a bachelor?

The birds lingered, staring into space with their melancholy eyes, as if they carried in their pupils all the tears of the world, including my mother's; especially the tears she'd held back since 1946, since the day my father married Kamar, the young teenage girl from Bône who hailed from an aristocratic Ottoman family, and who was capable of tracing – and flaunting – her family tree back to a Turkish corsair ancestor. Kamar, the owner and beneficiary of those 19 pure platinum Sicilian clocks nobody had ever laid eyes on.

As it happened, Kamar took her cue from Nadia, who was her aunt as well as Omar's mother and the one who had made up that story about the corsair ancestor and his 19 clocks. She was fascinated by her. Kamar imitated Nadia in every respect. The women were first cousins.

The birds carried in their eyes the tears which my mother had held back when she'd been sitting on top of one of her suitcases late at night in the icy cold, total darkness of Khroub railway station. When I – or my older brother, or my younger brother Zygote – stood by her side, observing her despite the veil that hid her entire face apart from her eyes, stealing glances while listening out for the sounds of the approaching train that suddenly made its deafening entry into the station, spouting jets of smoke, piercing the silence and shrouding the small station's platforms in thick fog.

After I reached fifty, I started spending time in Constantine on a more regular basis. I spent whole evenings with Omar. And when the bottles of whisky and wine from Mascara and Médéa had taken their effect, everything started to flow back into my memory, which was cluttered with Omar's family history and my own. I had bought the old family home and would often come to stay for long periods of time. As I got older, I needed that house, the Constantine weather and Omar's company. We dwelled on our memories like the pair of old bachelors that we were. When very young, we had struck a pact and decided that we would never get married! Never have children! Why? I've never fully understood. We often spoke about Mr Baudier and that passage by Victor Hugo which he had told us to read and re-read. It bothered us. We nursed such a profound love for Victor Hugo! But these words of praise for the guillotine that had arrived at the docks in Algiers to 'civilise' the Algerians…

My memories waylaid me, and I began to remember standing there while the train gradually came to a stop; my mother rushing to get her luggage so that I wouldn't see the tears running down her cheeks as the conductor blew his whistle with all his might. My mother was pretending to hurry, holding her suitcase in one hand and dragging me along by the other, running towards the first-class carriage, without a word, silent, calm, as if she were dead – or rather, as if her body were now devoid of life – with the white, raw silk inside her veil. It was as if she was being swallowed up by the earth she was trampling, vanishing, leaving no trace of her existence, because nothing mattered any more, apart from her suitcase and my hand, which she clutched so hard it started to hurt. I only had eyes for her veiled face, trying to read the magnitude of the sadness that had struck her in it, without any tangible results.

I couldn't help staring at her as the train sped towards the village she had left many years earlier with my father and my elder brother, Zahir, who had taken me to football matches and boxing bouts, introduced me to pornography and to books by a certain André Gide. And who, much to my distress, all too soon left me behind to deal with that infernal monozygotic twin brother of mine (even my mother had started calling him by his nickname, Zygote).

Suddenly, I stopped looking at her and found myself surrounded by noises, voices and by a sort of restlessness that quickly gave way to a fascination with the bustle, the panting of the steam engine, the sound of the wheels on the tracks, and the screeching of the carts that the station porter was pulling towards the tiny station's concourse. Then that horrible silence descended over the compartment once more and we sat down in our berths; my mother switched off the lights and we thundered into the world, into a frightening nothingness.

I very quickly fell in love with my young stepmother, who never stopped flirting with me, arousing my desires, and whose hairy pubis I could make out at the point where her thighs converged through her light, crumpled, silken nightgown. When she woke up, her eyes were sallow, her body on fire, her gait unsteady, and she always seemed – at least as far as I was concerned – enshrouded in mystery, to the point where I never stopped asking myself whether she had ever really loved my father, or if she were secretly in love with Zahir, my older brother.

My father's store was spacious. The midday sun was at its strongest

and the heat had reached its peak. There was a strong smell of cin-
namon everywhere. The account books were stacked so high that
they were waging war on the ceiling. The invoices were also piled
up higgledy-piggledy. Inks. Fabrics. Wood carvings. The antique
inkwell that father had purchased at the bazaar in Tehran. The
sharp pincers of boredom: the impression that a plant was sprout-
ing its shoots through my spinal cord. I fuck a whore who some-
times drops in to see me at the store. She takes my hand and pushes
it into her sex. Sticky fluid oozes from the longitudinal wound,
washing out all the humus, all the grass and all the plasma she
conceals within her.

Disgust. Nausea. The rotund curve of her belly. Frozen finger-
tips. Vibrating air that warps in places. The anarchy and chaos of
sex. The clitoris like a metal tube, while the vagina keeps spewing
out congealed sticky liquid. Betrayal by the senses: I watch the
distorted, wizened, shrunken passers-by through the frosted glass.
Confused senses! Where is the hole, the orifice, the crack? I vomit
and weep. Unhappiness is saffron-yellow and anxiety is green.
Maybe it's me Kamar loves. I was afraid then of falling into the
trap of arrogance and complacency, all the more so since my pride
knew no bounds.

The plane, like an arrow soaring towards its target. Unflinch-
ing. Like Zeno's arrow. Moving. Unmoving. Moving…

Chapter XI

THE MULBERRY TREE fascinated me in same way that Barbary figs fascinated Si Mustafa, Omar's grandfather, and Omar himself, who always wore a discreet little chain with a golden effigy of a Barbary fig around his neck. It was in that mythical tree that on one occasion – why I cannot recall – Omar and I made love to the twins, Mounia and Dounia. We usually carried on with the twins at one of Si Mustafa's summer homes.

I had dozed off, when, at dusk, I opened my eyes. I saw the sun brush the top branches of the mulberry tree and daub them a delicate pink, as if painting the top of a wall with a soft, wan, orangey or, rather, copper-coloured, light. The tiles seemed sullied by a reddish substance; the birds had vacated the roof, and slightly lower, level with the west-facing wall that the sun hadn't yet struck, the hue was still quite purple. The beams of sunlight began to converge into parallel lines and drain away, sucked back by the perspective towards a point beyond the wall.

I left both of the window shutters open. The mulberry tree was whispering; the birds were warbling.

Outside, the riots had reached their climax.

The birds in my garden reminded me of the ones Fernand Yveton spoke of in his correspondence with his wife Béa while he awaited execution, letters which I knew by heart. Like that general's contradictory letters during the colonial era: that mix of cruelty and tenderness had always astonished me. The birds flew up from the lilacs and the red-thorned Barbary figs, and those in the reeds began all of a sudden to shoot up out of the bulrushes beside a bubbling spring. The clouds were now falling into the tangle of wires tapping into the streetlights.

Yveton remembered this each time he passed the seafront bird market on his way from Barbarossa prison to the courthouse. He remembered, with a deal of pride, how his advice had been sought on the art of handling the small mirror that he lovingly and attentively polished and used to capture the most beautiful birds. He couldn't offer any precise explanations, but was always ready to teach by example, carrying his iron-wire basket and his mirror, demonstrating some practical techniques. He had always been good with his hands and had become a metal mechanic once he had obtained his certificate, not long after he was expelled from secondary school for political reasons and pointed in the direction of an apprenticeship centre, where he had quickly turned out to be an excellent lathe operator.

At the age of eight, Yveton had seen proof that rich people did not have some devilish power that made them stronger than anyone else. During his childhood, when he went round to sell them sparrows, red-breasted robins and canaries, he had understood that the rich occupied one sphere in life, while the poor were in another. A desire to provoke this class of people led him to seduce the headmaster's daughter at his school, and he was subsequently put through a disciplinary hearing for his affront to good manners.

Fernand Yveton did his revision in the tiny vegetable garden that his mother tended and stayed there until the sun cast the shadows thrown by every object in the garden: the skeletal scarecrows; the battens of the old, battered boarding; the bits of fence that his mother moved each night to try and gain a few extra inches of land; the latticework sticks for catching birds outdoors; the heavy rope ladders that disappeared into the clouds; the collection of miscellaneous objects half-eaten by sea-rust; the animal hides crumbling away like blackened, mouldy sieves; the tiles slippery with wet moss; the patched-up wooden milk buckets. It was around this time that he began to develop a taste for football and tango.

When he played football, he realised that the ball's movement and trajectories were connected to the flow of time, which transformed that agglomeration of movements and actions imprinted in the air into units – where seconds, minutes and hours passed by over and over again on that same yellowing strip of life, causing space to crumble and be reduced to nothing.

He now had nothing left to show from those early important days, having withdrawn into a state of hibernation, cutting himself off from the world, rarely even speaking to his lawyer and instead writing long letters to Béa and asking after his cat's health and mood. A week after he was hideously tortured, he couldn't stop hearing the nasal twang of his torturers' voices and couldn't stop seeing the birds of his childhood, the images of his town and the photographs of the crucial events in his life parade before his eyes.

Sometimes, Fernand dreamt of Béa's body – a body he explored as if searching not for an orgasm, for a liberating explosion or that diabolical obsession with penetration, but instead for some kind of absolution, purification and a total and absolute out-of-body experience. Sometimes, even when in the grip of a feverish dream, burning with desire, searching for the slit of Béa's sex in the tuft of tangled hair, striving to locate it with his fingers like a blind man feeling a lacy, delicate, flimsy piece of cloth; spreading the moist, silky wrinkles of her lips, then feverishly taking her, thrusting his member as deep inside her as possible, knocking against the wall of her womb with such unaccustomed violence, a sort of savagery even, hurting her, repeatedly ramming and slamming into her, hearing in his dream her moans, her wails, her groans, her heavy breathing; then thrusting even further inside her, as if he wasn't fucking her womb but her throat, out of which all this moaning and wailing emerged.

As if by doing all this, by wanting all this in such a confused and hurried manner, he was quenching not so much his desire for his wife, but expiating his fear of the slow ceremony that was unfolding before him in the presence of judges, lawyers, the executioner and his assistants, and perhaps even – unusually – the priest, whom he didn't want to see. The rain on the roof: the only noise in that narrow crack of life dominated by its own peculiar silence. On hearing the guards' strained voices, Yveton knew that night had now fallen and he checked once more on his watch that it was 9.45 pm. Every passing day that separated him from the trial, or the verdict, or the execution, was like a towel soaked in his own blood, so afraid was he of those unstoppable seconds.

It was a change from his talkative teenage years, when there had been football games at the time the swallows and black-birds flew into a frenzy, their singing doused by the sporadic summer showers. The last echoes of days glossed by the haze of the docks. The whorehouses he ran through with a football in his hands. The nice, tubercular prostitutes touting their wares and calling out, 'Come here, little one, come here! Go ahead and touch it. Don't be scared. I've got a silky pussy. You won't regret spending your pennies on me. Look at this wondrous slit. I'm a tart, a pretty tart. Look, little one… Cat got your tongue, huh. You can have a feel, it's not flabby like those of upper class ladies… A tart, my little one, and mine is the saliva that's going to wet your little cock… I'm a pretty tart, aren't I? And it's my saliva… What more could you possibly want?'

Those shanty-town street urchins, Europeans, Jews and Arabs, laughed such nonsense off, preferring to go and pilfer sweets from the patisseries in the modern part of the city, whose window displays looked like Egyptian sarcophagi. They dodged the fares by jumping onto moving trams to ride up into the heights of the city. From there, dizziness came all the more easily because there was a cliff covered in liquid, putrid refuse. There were domes as far as the eye could see. Frames, honeycombs and the ochre, white and blue-coloured roofs. The commotion in the terraces jutting out over the drop. A watermarked sheet of paper scribbled with pathetic drawings. The painted pieces of paper used to mask the puppeteer's faces as they told their stories. The stairs! The stairs of Algiers, which he used to run up and down all day long, and which had been the thrill of his childhood. And in his cell on death row, the fear, anguish and nostalgia helped the memories of those stairs come crashing through his mind and linger there for hours. Those marvellous Algiers stairs! Stairs that had been grafted on here and there to the body of the city, a city he had taken in with his eyes and his whole body as well, when he was a mischievous little boy.

Those stairs appeared before him as an amazing revelation, rising vertically and unexpectedly and rushing towards the sky. Horizontally, the stairs appeared to him like an animal ceaselessly pacing inside and around him, without respite or break, in helix-shaped circles, picking space apart and rending objects and people.

Thanks to the sea salt and the humidity, Algiers was often bathed in a plant-like ambiguity that sped up childhood restlessness and condemned it to sleeplessness, at the corner of green alleyways or dark-blue porches where, having made its way this far, there was a tinkling of the cobalt light and lasciviousness promised by any Arab and Jewish home that was open to the day and closed around the shade of the large black nails decorating the doors and the arabesque designs framing the windows. He – the poor white boy – had hung on to these wonderful memories up until the moment Fernand Meyssonnier, also know as Mr Algiers, thrust a hood over his head, plunging him into the emptiness we call death.

When the war got underway, Yveton had witnessed the looting of his Algerian friends' homes, the rape of neighbourhood girls, the daily disappearance of hundreds of people and the cold-blooded murder of innocents, and read the untimely declarations issued by the minister who would later refuse to grant him a pardon and would dispatch him to the guillotine, no less.

The newspaper headlines were edifying:

GENTLEMEN!
FRANCE REACHES
FROM FLANDERS TO THE CONGO

THERE MUST BE A RUTHLESS CLAMPDOWN
IN THIS PART OF FRANCE!

THREE HUNDRED *FELLAGHA*
WIPED OUT IN THE
CONSTANTINE REGION

It was at this point that Fernand Yveton, a fellow traveller in the Algerian Communist Party, decided to get involved in the war, choosing to side with the poor, the colonised and the outcasts: the white trash, the despised Jews and the hungry Arabs.

From the window of my home in Algiers I could see the latticework of the roof. Even though night had fallen, it continued to let the light in, as if the wood were serving as a light conductor, storing it up amidst the smell of paint softened by the warmth that was swelling in burning waves, not from the sky, but from other whitewashed roofs and terraces. The wood sent into the room I used as an office a beam of brighter, deadlier light that reminded me of the countless deaths, crimes, massacres, genocides, betrayals – the internecine, fratricidal and fundamentalist wars, or those who had simply died of natural causes, as they say, or accidentally.

The parallelism of dark thoughts, of hallucinations and destinies refracted during the early hours of the morning. I began to reminisce about the war against colonialism that Omar and I had taken part in with such passion and sincerity. I was appalled, stricken with chronic grief and melancholy as I watched Algerian soldiers, of all people, savagely putting down those angry riots during that mild month of October 1988. I ached all over, as if I had been torn apart. From time to time, I heard a sharp explosion; sometimes a salvo of gunfire. The growing anxiety and strain of the following days began to wear me down; I was powerless to do anything. I had a wild desire to rush down into the street and join the riots. The widely repeated, disgusting headlines in the official newspapers read:

ORDER HAS BEEN
RESTORED THROUGHOUT
THE ENTIRE COUNTRY

And that man who had had his testicles crushed and whom I had spent a whole night patching up. I was also contending with the permanent anxiety I felt at the thought that they might come at any moment to arrest me, not only for what I had tried to do at the hospital, where I served as a general practitioner, but for many other reasons. This impalpable and invisible monstrosity floating in the air forced me to live in a terrifying state of constant hallucination.

The telephone lines never stopped buzzing between Omar and me. To no avail! I was frustrated because words had lost all meaning. We were desperate. But the worst was the sense of shame, the self-loathing.

At night, while I slept I would hear – even at the hospital – the rasping voice of Aunt Fatima, our old maid who used to give me the worst frights of my childhood when she ordered us to go to sleep, if my brothers, my sisters or I made the slightest noise – all of us save Zygote of course, for he enjoyed preferential treatment. What little sleep I did get was restless. Hateful awakenings. Such dark thoughts, childhood fears, macabre dreams (Aunt Fatima, our old maid, was run over by the six o'clock morning tram, while the fritters she had gone out to buy had remained horribly intact) and recurring fixations ran in parallel.

All these thoughts and hallucinations started to refract at the beginning of each new, rotten day, which was not so much milky as wine-dark. Even the branches of the mulberry tree, which were usually so phosphorescent before sunrise, looked tired and shrivelled. The tram was green. I was seven or eight years old at the time. I liked jumping on when it was moving. I don't know whether Ali – also known as 'Nightmare Face' – ever saw it. Obviously not. Why 'Nightmare Face' anyway? He was rather handsome. A nickname. But what did that nickname hide? The manner in which they'd tortured him. They'd castrated him. Left him for dead. He would have been better off dead than having that mush between his legs now.

The trams when I was a kid had an electric trolley pole on top of the carriage that pointed up to the heavens. When the pole slipped off the overhead wires, the conductor quickly got out and tried to put it back in place. This could take a long time. We stood there mocking the poor guy because he wouldn't let us sneakily dodge the fare. That grotesque, obscene trolley pole! Waggling around all over the place!

During those listless mornings, between waking up and heading off to the hospital, everything came flooding back as if in some terrible loop. Maybe it was simply flashbacks to the dreams and nightmares I'd had during my few hours of sleep? But it happened all over again the next morning. Perhaps it was my fear of another day at the hospital, where I would have to perform at least a dozen, sometimes slapdash, operations. Some days, I realised that even after so many years in the operating room, I still couldn't take it casually. I always felt scared before an operation. The same nerves every time. The same panic when faced with the white sheets. And above all that abominable, irrational, quasi-hysterical fear of blood. The worst thing for a surgeon. Miriam, who was my anaesthetist as well as my lover, never stopped teasing me about it. Everything would become muddled before an exhausting day of work. Everything came flooding back. Old memories and ideas came welling up... I tried keeping my hands busy.

Soaping up under the shower. Shaving. Making coffee. It was no use. Aunt Fatima, the maid, suffered for many hours. Those fritters, unscathed when they pulled them out from under the tram; she was obsessed with them. They were still warm, oily and crispy. She suffered for many hours. The firemen didn't arrive in time to help her. Her body had been sliced in half.

Logically speaking, Aunt Fatima should have died on the spot, especially since she was very old – even though no one knew her exact age. When someone asked her, she would invariably reply, 'I turned 20 one day and that's where I stopped. So I'm still 20, right?' She said it without laughing. She never laughed; she was always in a bad mood. A grumpy woman. But I really liked her. Nobody knew how she'd got her limp either, because no one had ever dared to ask. Would she even have deigned to answer?

When those disgraceful allegations about my mother's so-called adultery came out – adultery I had allegedly abetted – Aunt Fatima was mortified. She lost her fangs and immured herself behind a vast wall of silence. But my father didn't let go. Aunt Fatima was in convulsions for a long time under the tram. A vision of hell. Blood and entrails everywhere. The unbearable death rattles. There were a handful of snot-nosed brats who were trying to nick the fritters that were held together by a paper string. It was a blood-spattered vision of hell, with those entrails sticking out. I thought she would be stuck under that tram forever.

I opened the window just for something to do, since I had no desire to return to the devastated city in its state of siege. Nor did I want to go back to the hospital where I might find Ali 'Nightmare Face' with those enormous bandages between his legs. So I opened the window.

The plane was motionless…

Chapter XII

AFTER A FEW SECONDS, the mulberry tree managed to poke some of its branches through the open window into the room, almost timidly, by which time it was getting dark and muggy, without doubt due to the summer drought that had lasted for two or three months. Nightmare after nightmare, the memories came flooding back; all thanks to my having been surrounded by the pervasive atmosphere of the civil war (the October riots in Algiers in 1988) and to my wading through blood; all that operating on patients left, right and centre at a hellish tempo.

If Aunt Fatima took a long time to die, so did my grand-mother, though in a different manner. Without suffering. With decorum. I have kept an old, sepia-coloured, blurry photograph of her taken on the day she passed away. It was elaborately staged. She had a malicious air to her and wore her formal madder-coloured velvet dress; an ample traditional gown. She wore a complicated hat on her head, which was cone-shaped and had elaborate tiers. She'd asked to be adorned with all her jewellery, and since she didn't consider her own sufficient or extravagant enough, she'd borrowed some from her neighbours.

Groomed, and decked in splendid jewellery, she was laid on her gigantic bed, which was surrounded by a mosquito net as well as silk and cotton drapery. She insisted a photographer be sent for immediately. The little fellow arrived, carrying his dismantled equipment concealed in a wicker basket, since he worked cash in hand, without a licence. He was almost certainly a nationalist militant who had been banished to our town (part of a widespread policy of internally displacing dissidents favoured by the colonial authorities of the time) who had been denied the right to any legitimate work or to receive any help from anyone and was instead obliged to sign a specific register at the police station twice a day; once in the morning and once in the evening. Knowing the old woman was at death's door, he took the camera parts out of the basket and put them together in the blink of an eye, and, setting his tripod up a few yards from the bed, pressed the button, thus immortalising that horrible old woman, or rather immortalising her malice, which was the stuff of legend – the way she'd held her husband under her thumb, that rag-doll-like little man with blue eyes and rosy cheeks, who, though virtually beardless, had had the stomach, time and audacity to father a dozen children by her, one of whom was my father.

This was the photograph of the grandmother who had marred my childhood, but who had nonetheless fascinated me enough to make me sneak off behind my mother's back to watch her for hours on end. A photograph that was yellowish on the back and brown on the front, printed on the kind of paper that hasn't existed for years, showing my enormous grandmother, who was so obese she could barely walk and whom the women of the house had to carry from room to room, or rather from her bedroom to the kitchen, where she would supervise the preparation of various delicacies (pastries, sorbets, Turkish delight, halva, cordials and orgeat syrup) which she would taste by sticking her right index finger into them while they were cooking. This finger was always painted with henna, and she would wash it several times a day, because, aside from being obese and duplicitous, she was also obsessed with cleanliness.

Grandmother was only interested in cooking, and thanks to her constant dipping of her hennaed forefinger into stews, sauces, grilled meats, steamed chicken, braised fish, pastries, pasties, couscous, treacle and honey, she had come to weigh almost 24 stone. Another photograph showed her sitting cross-legged on her bed, leaning against a dozen cushions made out of embroidered percale, with that absurd and hilarious cone-shaped, madder taffeta hat on her head. Her plaited hair was so very black, and naturally black at that! According to my mother, my grandmother had never dyed her hair (even though she was crazy about lotions and shaving powders – which she herself prepared, assuming an alchemist's arrogance in the process – wonderful red lipsticks, stunning mascara, kohl, incredibly rare Arabic gum and so on), even though she had sailed past her 80th birthday and suffered from a whole host of incurable illnesses: diabetes, hypertension, uraemia, proteinuria, gout and phlebitis. Despite my grandmother's age, her obesity and these painful conditions, her jet-black plaits in this photograph made her look like a young girl.

But it wasn't only the black plaits that made her look younger, for she had managed to keep her face slender, smooth and rosy despite the misshapen body she disguised under frills and flounces. That didn't prevent her face from looking stern and authoritative in the photograph, filled with a self-satisfied malice. How she had made my mother suffer! Oh, that brown-coloured photograph where her face is slender and her cheeks are aglow with a youthful rosy tinge; that joke of an ancestress who struck such a natural pose, wearing that pompous, arrogant expression in front of the old militant-turned-photographer. She feared neither death nor any of the people around her; she had no time for God, or anyone else in her family for that matter – save for that moron, Uncle Hocine, who was just as fat as she was, a mama's boy who clung to her skirts and had made nothing of his life, happy to follow his mother around the kitchen, kissing, touching, caressing and hugging her for the whole world to see.

The communist Fernand Yveton was also an obsession of mine for the rest of my life. Even after I grew up, I never stopped thinking about him, re-reading the newspapers of the day that told the stories of his pathetic fate. I usually wound up phoning Omar, back when we were students in Algiers, and later when Omar passed through Algiers briefly on business, so that we could go and roam the bars of the city and get absolutely plastered. Our words misted over in our mouths and the glasses fell from our hands. We were alone with our nostalgia, our grief still unprocessed, our determined but incomprehensible bachelorhood, our untamed rowdiness. The Algiers bars where we wet our whistles and drowned our sorrows, and where the alcohol tasted like formalin. I knew formalin from the hospital, where I poked around in human suffering for many long hours. Omar started to cry and I tried my best not to follow suit. But I ended up crying anyway. At our age, we must have cut a sorry sight as we continued to nurse our hang-ups and push ourselves into the margins. Our lives had come down to this bar and this sawdust-strewn floor. At the height of drunkenness, it seemed to me that Omar's eyes had become like a railway station concourse full of emptiness and expectation.

Omar asked, 'Why is going on benders in ordinary bars always better than getting pissed at my place or yours?'

We were dead drunk! But fully aware that we had once more cocked a snook at convention… Omar never spoke about the fates of either his father or younger brother when we drank in those bars.

As for me, I was obsessed with Fernand Yveton's fate: he stood out as an example, perhaps because he was innocent and my mother had been so fixated on him – to the point where she began to identify with him, comparing the way in which she had been unfairly accused of adultery with the way Yveton had been sentenced to death and guillotined for a crime he didn't commit.

I forgot about Omar and his guilty conscience, his steadfast dedication to bachelorhood, as well as those inextricably entwined memories of our family life. I forgot about our youthful depravities, my own family's nauseating quagmire. Instead, I became obsessed with history's twists, its U-turns and its horrors. History, or rather an accumulation of trivial details. This process of stratification. That meticulous arrangement of human suffering. Nothing more.

THE EUROPEAN PUBLIC SEES THE EXECUTION OF THE COMMUNIST TERRORIST AS THE ULTIMATE PROOF OF FRANCE'S DETERMINATION TO PUNISH THE TERRORISTS

Fernand Yveton hadn't behaved like some of the other natives: the Ali Chekkals, the Alain Mimouns, the Abdessalems (Abdessalem was a rather mediocre but hunky tennis player who was a sell-out as well as a sleaze). A shameless bunch of careerists one and all, who sold their loyalties to the highest bidder or, in some cases, hedged their bets.

**CALM HAS BEEN RESTORED TO
THE WHOLE COUNTRY
AFTER THE ALGIERS RIOTS
OF DECEMBER 1960.**

The war had been terrible. Some luxury hotels had been blown up, leaving hundreds dead and injured under the rubble, innocent people for the most part who had been caught in the maelstrom of the revolutionary uprising. Numerous hip cafés, fine restaurants and nightclubs had been laid to waste by the Organisation's bombs. (After the end of the war, Omar and I learnt that one of the eccentric twins had belonged to an exclusively female underground network of bombers in Algiers, with members from all walks of life – Hassiba Ben Bouali, Zohra Drif, Djamila Boupacha, Annie Steiner, Raymonde Peschard, Jeanne Messica and one of the twins – Mounia or Dounia?) Trains were blown apart by mines while crawling through tunnels and rock faces, suddenly catapulted into the air, then turned into a solid mass of soft, turgid putty. Buses were sprayed with bullets, crumbling into a tangle of broken parts and human remains. Convoys of soldiers were trapped in surprise ambushes, refineries ravaged by fires (Mourepiane, Le Havre). Those were real bomb attacks! That was war!

**ANOTHER FRIEND OF FRANCE
IS MURDERED. THE BASHAGHA
ALI CHEKKAL WAS MOWN DOWN
BY A KILLER AT THE STADE DE
COLOMBES WHERE
THE FRENCH CUP FINAL
WAS BEING PLAYED WITH**

FC TOULOUSE BEATING SCO ANGERS 6–3.

In his cell, Fernand Yveton often dreamt about the poor white neighbourhood where he grew up, which bordered the shanty town populated by Arabs or Negroes or natives... Places he could no longer see clearly, that is to say visually, but recalled by smell: the breeze that converged on the squalid tenements came from the sea and the city, aggravating the already sickening stench of the open sewers, of rancid oil, of rank tiny fishes being fried, of urine trickling along the ground – itself a stamped-down mixture of porous asphalt, sand, pebbles – iron filings, mud, rotten vegetables, the remains of chickens that had been gutted and their entrails which had been thrown outside people's homes, tangy, sour fruit, beef that had been dried and salted by the brine that gnaws away at everything and makes it reek, detritus washed up by the sea that the children would collect in aluminium cans to play with, or sometimes even eat, and vomit that smelt strongly of alcohol, on which someone had thrown a handful of bran. Right in front of the shanty town's only bar. In addition, there was stagnant, silty water everywhere, yellowish excrement, salted cod hanging from wires stretched across the Arab, Negro, Maltese, Sicilian or Sardinian streets, and the pungent odour of hung, pickled anchovies. Under some ruins lay the decomposing bodies of cats that had been skinned by a sadist, an old soot-skinned sailor who silently stalked the surroundings of the spring where Yveton used to set his bird-traps as a boy. Everywhere the oppressive, musty smell of poverty, misery, sweat, fear, and the miasma of corpses and urine...

This built-up tension gave Yveton the impression of having sound waves and electrical currents running through his body, as if the blood that soaked the prison walls around him left its traces in his guts, chiselling away at him and coating him with a layer of rock salt, the sort used by the barbarians, which they didn't use to season their food, but to rub into the wounds of martyrs.

Yveton felt obliged not to give in to either surprise or distress in the eventuality that he was sentenced to death, not only for his own sake, but also because he had a vague hunch that such weakness on his part would have angered Béa. The sound of blood, blending with the snatches of sleep and coma, seemed to be absorbed by, or dissolve into, the glory of the broken, decapitated, maddened and castrated bodies by the simple cowardly act of those political string-pullers sitting in their plush offices.

Once more, Fernand Yveton was able to call to mind a range of flavours, smells and sensations, all thanks to the proximity of the bodies of his comrades imprisoned in the night who couldn't retreat to the safety of their own caves and their walls oozing with moisture and red paint. When the inevitable execution of a militant was announced, a murmur quickly spread through the entire prison, growing louder as it went.

Omar and I eventually reached a bitter conclusion: that all power was oppressive and unjust, and that the colonial class had simply been replaced by a nomenclature of bloodsucking Algerian *nababs*.

Back in the plane, Omar seemed to have calmed down.

The plane was beginning its descent.

Chapter XIII

FERNAND YVETON refused to call what he was feeling 'fear' because, rather confusingly, he associated that with sex, when Béa parted her thighs, taking him back to his teenage years when he thought he'd divined the meaning of life in the smells of the wealthy women to whom he sold his most beautiful canaries, travelling to the other side of his neighbourhood or even further afield, into the red-light district, where he would go and ogle the prostitutes with his friends of all different races.

BOMB EXPLOSION AT THE CASINO ON THE COAST ROAD KILLS SIXTY PEOPLE

Also present was the memory of an impossible kind of physical contact, which was re-assembling in dark recesses, through the bruised, wounded bodies lying in the haunted confines, permeating the dilapidated walls of all the prisons in the world, where the guillotine that stood inviolable in the courtyard never stopped working for a single second. He felt the need to plunge into the gloom of insomnia, into the torments of doubt and confusion, and put to one side all his foresight, lucidity and clear awareness of all the phenomena that were coalescing around him.

There were few objects in his cell, a box full of clothes, a few cans of food, one or two bananas, a handful of officially-approved magazines, the reading of which he considered a dreadful betrayal, but which he nonetheless read because they were the means by which he measured the lousy hope of saving his skin, when so many others before him had striven so hard and had ultimately failed.

That had certainly not been the case for the man who had walked past Yveton's cell one day at dawn, heading word-lessly for the scaffold. Yveton was, however, aware that some of his comrades-in-arms had given in to their fears, shouting, foaming at the mouth and pissing themselves when the screws dragged them towards the shining instrument of death, which was leaning against a low, moss-covered, peaceful country wall. This had infuriated their executioner, Mr Algiers! Yveton also knew that the first two men to be guillotined, Ahmed Zabana and Mohammed Ferradj, who was both blind and disabled, had reacted to the guillotine differently. Zabana had com-ported himself with dignity and scorned his fate. Ferradj, on the other hand, had given in to panic. And his fate was all the more heart-wrenching for it!

The condemned man felt the urge to howl like a wolf. Inside, he was in pain. On that fateful morning, he had had the impres-sion that he was crawling through the entirety of human cos-mography until he reached the old, dimly-lit haunts of his childhood, which was swallowed up in blissful sleep while he lay stretched out on his kapok mattress, where he dreamt he was exploring Béa's body, as if in search not of an orgasm, the liber-ating explosion or the brutal, savage, hellish desire to penetrate her, but of an absolute immortality, so fearful was he of death.

All condemned men awaiting either a pardon or their exe-cution were lodged three to a cell. The cells were small, only

30 square feet, and were foul, run-down and equipped with squat toilets. In some cases, this insalubrious proximity to one another made the prisoners very aggressive and violent. By virtue of always eating, sleeping and defecating together they went mad, losing all sense and reason, recovering their wits only to lose them once more.

One of these death cells was home to Taleb Abderrahmane, a young chemistry student who had been assigned the task of making bombs for the resistance right up until the moment he was arrested and sentenced to death. He was only 21 years old and his cellmates were older than him. One day, the three men argued over a trifle. Taleb Abderrahmane, the Organisation's chemist, found himself alone against the other two, who subsequently flew into a rage. They forced him to defecate and eat his own excrement. Truth be told, his torturers were jealous of him because Abderrahmane was a scholar, while they were illiterate.

Three days after this horrible act of sadism, Taleb Abderrahmane was guillotined. A few months later, his tormentors were pardoned.

Omar's opinion on this was the following: 'No comment!'

It was the first and last time we ever discussed Taleb Abderrahmane's ordeal.

A few years prior to sharing this flight with Omar, we had spent a summer together in the old family home in Constantine. Just the two of us. I had had much to say about my job as a surgeon at the hospital in Algiers, my neurosis about my family, and about the incestuous quagmire my feudalistic father had dumped me in. He may have always been a nationalist. He may have spent 12 years in a colonial gaol. He may have been erudite. (He used the Tunis-Constantine bus service he owned and operated to exchange French books for Arabic ones, at no charge.) But deep down, he was an absolute swine. He hadn't collaborated with the enemy like Omar's father had, but he'd been a cruel and perverse father who'd destroyed all his wives, mistresses and children. Including me.

One pleasant afternoon when Omar and I were sat in the garden drinking whisky, I put it to him: 'Why are we still wading through all our set-backs and defeats all these years after Independence? Why do we still not have a calendar, a diary, an almanac? Isn't it just our way of running away from time? This infamous fate that gives us such a good reputation? Which would be of no use to you, since you're a mere photo-copy of that fucking collective destiny. You forsake your ances-tors and the heavy burden of their past, but are nonetheless fascinated by them to the point where you take pride in them, to the point where they stick to your skin. Where everything revolves around time and space, neither of which we learnt to wield, thanks to the vertiginous scale of history… For the past few days I have wanted to understand your silence – you never say anything any more. You do nothing but stare at things, off into the distance as far as the eye can see! I have often over-heard you mumbling and babbling to yourself when you're alone, but you prefer listening to me rattle on about my life – our life! – going off on tangents, from pillar to post, clouding the real issues, forgetting what matters, and, like always, I fall into your trap, since I always catch myself in that act of nar-rating my life using awkward, inadequate words. That's why I cheat, I feel obliged to embellish it all with stylistic effects, peppering it with the usual flourishes typical of this sort of situation. Tricks, what else!

'And so you casually steal snatches of conversations here, snatches of conversations there, digging up my past, my family, the petty details of my wretched life, draining me. I feel like an idiot. You're wrong to believe in all that nonsense I keep spouting! Take my older brother Zahir for example, who didn't really die while dead drunk on my mother's prayer mat. No, that was a lie. A myth, a tall tale. He was murdered by the Red Hand. Or rather the French Secret Services. You, on the other hand, never venture any lies, since you never bother saying anything at all. Well, that's easy! Apart from when it concerns your father and brother… Tell me Omar: why have we become old bachelors?'

Omar parried fiercely, 'Does that bother you? Do you long for marriage, a swarm of children? Have you forgotten our pledge? You're not in any position to ask me such a question. You stayed single because you were simply averse to marriage. Your father had four wives, two thousand mistresses and something like fifty children!'

I said nothing. His argument was irrefutable.

Then he added, 'When you got back from the bush, you lied about being impotent – or was it infertile? I forget which! – just to avoid getting married. Have you forgotten about that?'

Waking up, having soaked in the last rays of sunshine, Nana the cat started running off in all directions. Bit by bit, the commotion began to spread, repopulating the very same places that had been deserted for so many hours, which were now suddenly besieged by a whole fauna of insects, birds and the hedgehog, to whom I had taught a sort of Morse code, and who reacted to my whistle. By dint of listening to it, he had developed a deep love of music. I took advantage of the silence to tease the cat, who was stretching to shake off the rest of her melancholy. 'You're nothing but a scaredy-cat, aren't you! Come over into the shade, away from the sun.' Omar suddenly burst out laughing hysterically. He asked, 'How's Mozart?' I made no reply. I was stung by the hurtful truths he had flung at me.

I ignored his question, knowing full well that he was trying to provoke me. Should I tell him about my correspondence with Dounia – or Mounia – during my time in the bush? No! It wasn't the right moment. And the cat, who no longer had any shade, didn't want to be bothered any more. She managed to escape from me to go and stalk the birds around the garden, who had begun their daily hubbub; between them and the cat was the leafy bliss of the trees at this silk-smooth time of day when the swallows came flocking in from all directions and acrobatically avoided Nana's clutches, before heading towards the mulberry tree or brushing past the proud, stately Barbary figs, whose stiffness was reminiscent of sculptures by Zadkine and Giacometti. From afar, we poked fun at Nana, who was stuck in warrior mode and utterly incapable of catching anything, as if – once her instincts had been distorted – all that remained of the hunter's atavism was the apparent mechanism, devoid of any capacity to act – rendering her useless, laughable.

After that, night fell quickly, spilling its ink like a frightened cuttlefish. I had lost my spark and was breathless and upset when confronted with the end of that day, which only increased my distress.

Then I remembered the way my father used to stand right in the middle of the courtyard during my childhood. Domineering, obnoxious and above all exceedingly childish, very touching in fact, encumbered by his four wives, his 50-odd kids, his numerous affairs and his countless mistresses dotted around the world. I had envied Omar, whose father was monogamous, faithful and loving, even sending his wife Nadia a bouquet of roses every day at four o'clock on the dot. A shame that he had wound up playing the role of a double agent, who died grief-stricken because no one knew where his youngest son – a zealous, active member of the OAS between 1961 and 1962 – had been buried.

My relationship with Omar was turbulent but wholly indispensable. Dogged memories of my teenage years: the rumble of the city fading out once one set foot in the garden, even when a light summer haze spread through the air clouded with the smoke emanating from the amber incense sticks my mother would place all around the courtyard to keep the insects at bay. The muggy garden air even infiltrated the electric lamps in the kitchen, where my mother and the maids were busy preparing dinner while the steam fogged up the windows, turning them opaque.

I then went back to my room and resumed reading General Bugeaud's letters, as if asking for more punishment, delving into the depths of horror, which I found soothing, as it seemed to lift all restrictions on me. Veins raw from the mix of words, flying low under the radar of my consciousness, on the fringes of sleep, like a sort of coma packed with petals of yellow and transparent roses. Were these the effects of the nostalgia I had always nursed inside?

Now an adult, I was sickened by the horrors perpetrated by the colonial power in the past, as well as by the present-day atrocities committed by my own country's potentates. As if this country were irremediably doomed to a tragic fate.

Even Victor Hugo had ventured to say, '*What France lacks in Algeria is a little barbarism. The Turks were quick about it, sure-footed, they pushed their limits; they were experts at slicing heads off."*

CALM HAS BEEN RESTORED THROUGHOUT THE ENTIRE COUNTRY AFTER THE RIOTS OF OCTOBER 1988.

The birds had meanwhile gathered on three or four trees in the garden, as if they looked down on the others, perhaps because they were not as lush.

Thus the rectangle formed by the dark green window separated into two parts: a cherry-red rectangle – my swollen eyelids – and an olive-green rectangle – the lush mulberry tree. Suddenly, I pricked my ears up to the voices of the birds, fleeting to start with, but soon swelling. When sleep began to take a hold of my mind, I felt that an imperceptible change had taken place; despite the fact that – when all was said and done – the air was still the same. It was just the transition between the end of the night and sunrise. Then this: the birds began to answer each other hesitantly and intermittently at a barely audible frequency, as though they were having second thoughts and stuttering, then swiftly taking heart until their perfectly pitched songs rose up from deep inside the mulberry tree and then from every tree in the garden. But the clearest harmonies of all came from the giant mulberry tree, whose branches continued to claw at my bedroom windows.

The melody's crescendo was soft and sweet and silky, and was promptly followed by a genuine, swelling concerto full of improvisation. The initial concerto gradually turned into a symphony, sometimes dissonant, sometimes harmonious, occasionally extremely precise. Then the musical and spatial arrangements

change — drastically even — at extraordinary speed. In one direc-
tion the horizon would be stained by a greenish streak, and in the
other the musical tumult reached its deafening climax. It was as
if the old world, struggling and unravelling in its slow, difficult
march, had acquired a new lease of life, reinvigorated by this sym-
phony of birds that sounded as if it were being performed on old
instruments grown rusty with the morning dew. My tame hedge-
hog began rolling on the ground as if drunk on music.

Then the dawn flooded the whole room with light. The early
morning brightness took hold in every corner, angle and object,
even the most insignificant.

The plane was preparing to land.

Chapter XIV

UNLIKE MY MOTHER, my father was a naturally talented fighter, as though his rural upbringing had instilled a terrible stubbornness in him, an ironclad fanaticism and an unbounded hunger for life. He took an interest in everything and his curiosity knew no limits. Nothing escaped him and he was always on the alert. When he went back to his village for a year and spotted the car that belonged to the wealthiest settler in the district, he immediately phoned the United States and ordered an incredibly luxurious dark-green car. The settler almost died of jealousy.

He really did take an interest in all forms of knowledge. Science and politics were of special fascination to him. Though he'd never set foot in a school, he was remarkably fluent in several languages, having always known how to keep busy each time he was put in prison for the same political reasons. He'd joined the nationalist movement at an early age. He'd spent a dozen years in prison. He loved books. He sent French language books to Tunisia and exchanged them for Arabic ones, thanks to the daily bus service he ran between Constantine and Tunis. There and back. He'd therefore been able to set up two vast libraries in the two countries. Free public libraries at a time when almost 100 per cent of the population in both French colonies was illiterate.

In our eyes, my father exuded an aura of erudition: his

pockets were always stuffed with books and scholarly publications. He sometimes even lectured on various history, philosophy or theology books in front of a small group of friends, but never made the slightest reference to the mediocre poems he composed in honour of Kamar, his second wife, who was barely pubescent at the time of her marriage and with whom he was madly in love (though I had strong suspicions about this, believing that he loved her not for her beauty, which he was incapable of fully appreciating, but rather for her lineage, which could be traced back to that famous corsair ancestor of hers). He called his friends as witnesses to the decadence of the Arabs, then got all worked up and called them a bunch of cowards. He frightened me. I will never forget those fits of rage, which he would direct against my mother, my brothers and me. He would take to throttling us with the brute force and savagery of a madman. He would stop for a few moments to catch his breath and dip his head in a pail of water brought to him by one of the maids, who was always at his beck and call, and with whom my father was carrying on an affair in full view of everyone. The beatings could last for hours on end. For absolutely no reason.

Now the old family home belonged to me. Since they had no love for the house, I had bought my brothers and sisters out. I had commissioned Omar to restore the house to its original glory. My grandfather had built that house a few years before perishing in the fire that ravaged his shop during the *Mawlid* festivities. Omar put his heart into the restoration because it was a very beautiful house and he knew how much I had loved my grandfather.

From time to time, Miriam, my anaesthetist, accompanied me to this place that was haunted by so many memories and hardships. Whenever she saw Miriam arrive with me, Nana would run off and spend the night outside. Out of modesty? Out of jealousy?

One summer evening, when we were dining together, Miriam unexpectedly took hold of my hand and led me into the garden under the giant mulberry tree. She shoved me to the ground and jumped on top of me. The fragrance of the night blended in with the sour smell of the mulberries hanging from the branches. Miriam was in total charge of the situation, removing her see-through dress with a single, quick, furtive gesture. She lay down naked on the grass under the mulberry tree, whose odour had seeped into my head through the pores of my skin, which was sticky by now – as if the mulberry had spilled its thick, viscous sap on me. The clouds were circling above our heads like a swarm of hornets, as though they were descending out of the tree, while, lower down, we could sense other clouds against our bodies, gathering into layers I could almost touch and feel with my fingertips. I saw birds spring from the branches with wings that looked as if they were the wrong way round. The birds appeared to be unhinged, irascible: perhaps because they had been frightened by our unexpected presence under the tree at this time of night. Miriam was stretched out with her legs spread as if she had been quartered.

I responded to her demands with unusual callousness. She wrapped her legs around my waist and locked my neck in a tight embrace; her violence laced with wounded pride. We hung there beneath the mulberry, a verdant vessel that kept reaching for the sky. The night wore on and became even more ink-like until the leaves stopped rustling and the birds ceased their cries, angrily sinking into sleep. A strange smell began to slowly override that of the night and the mulberry, spreading to the place where we were making love, filling every air pocket, every nook and cranny: the stench of spoilt fruit (IN OUR COUNTRY NATURE IS STILL NATURAL. ORANGES IN ALGERIA ACTUALLY TASTE LIKE ORANGES. OUR BRAND IS OUR BOND: PULPA!) and of overripe cheese (FRANCE PRODUCES MORE THAT 500 TYPES OF CHEESE. GIVE IN TO YOUR GALLIC INSTINCTS – EAT CHEESE!) – made with milk that had gone off. I sniffed the air. So did Miriam. I felt as if I were metamorphosing under the mulberry. Some part of Miriam, something vague and ill-defined, got under my nails. The smell came from far away, perhaps from one of the sweltering, sticky tropical countries my father had often visited.

MADAGASCAR
12-7-1953

It was as if something were rising from her vulva, filling every fibre of my being down to my toes with fire. I heard my voice cease to resonate in the air. It was as if it had simply left me, or rather, as if I could listen to the silence leaving my throat at the right moment, in a flash, just before the words came to halt.

While I was still going down on her, I raised my head and felt Miriam's eyes upon me. 'What's wrong? What's happened to you?' she asked. I pulled away. Picked up large handfuls of the squashed, mouldy berries scattered around the gigantic mulberry tree and stuffed them into her vagina. She staggered back in shock and surprise and ran towards the house, which was shrouded in darkness. We went upstairs to our room. She immediately got out a cigarette to conceal her discomfort and bewilderment; as was her habit, she rummaged around for a long time looking for something to light it with, chancing upon an orange lighter with the name of some petroleum derivative (NAPHTALIA) written on it. The lighter had been left next to the old lamp, in the middle of the small, purplish circles that had been engraved on the wooden surface of the desk, which was also an antique. She pressed down on the lighter and drew the flame near to the end of her cigarette.

Her voice seemed to be coming out of the thick ribbons of smoke that had settled over the room; perhaps because she was more hoarse than usual. She stopped enunciating the letters each time she took a drag on her cigarette, inhaling the smoke greedily, then blowing out gusts of Virginia tobacco, the odour of which I found bland and nauseating.

A grey rain began to fall, lashing the leaves of the mulberry tree, which already looked more aquatic than during the dry weather, poking its branches into the room, almost as if seeking shelter from the elements. But Miriam promptly hurried over to shut the windows with an irritated gesture, as if she could no longer withhold her resentment of the tree, which I had so often told her about before she saw it with her own eyes. Miriam was angry with me for interrupting our carnal act under the tree and for stuffing her most private parts full of mouldy berries.

The summer rain was now violently thrashing the leaves, emitting a tinny, almost piercing din, vaguely reminiscent of the noise Uncle Jaloul's wooden leg made when he walked down the cobbled alleyway to his shop. He was my father's business partner, who one day hanged himself because my father had forced him into bankruptcy out of sheer, unwarranted malice. I came across the body – I was still a child then – hanging from a length of rope. Uncle Jaloul's wooden leg had carried on swinging, never coming to a stop. That's another nightmare whose memory is still strong. Or the dragging sound of Aunt Fatima's shuffle on the ground-floor paving stones; as if it was the same rain that 15 years ago had soaked into the skeletal bones of my Jewish stepmother, who had been bedridden in that large house for a long time until her frazzled body – where cancer had taken root – was reduced to sinews and there was little left of the poor woman apart from her great big eyes, her toothless mouth, her chapped, grainy skin, and her large, bald head, which resembled that of a giant insect.

That sorry bag of bones who had once been a very beautiful woman, a magnificently talented dressmaker with a gift for haute couture and stormy love affairs, who went so far as to defy her community's intractable stance on the matter of mixed marriages. She had fallen madly in love with my well-heeled father to whom she was married with great pomp, even though there was no marriage certificate, nor any document proving her conversion to Islam. Which she didn't know. Even though the family had persisted in calling her 'the Jewess' after her marriage in a show of disdain. Henriette Gozlan was cheated on, scoffed at, diddled and finally rejected after a few years. Then Henriette had been diddled by death, which didn't want her, for she bore her affliction for many long, miserable years.

Of my three stepmothers, Henriette was my favourite, and I had looked after her myself when she was diagnosed, cramming one oncology textbook after another. All in vain! It was the rain that finally washed my Jewish stepmother clean of my father's abject stain, ridding her of all the grief she had been subjected to since the very first day my father had caught sight of her in a sewing workroom where she was fitting my mother – freeing her from that foetid bog, once and for all unclogging the drain, allowing those sordid waters of family histories, those listless waters of life, to wash away.

Making a 90 degree turn, the plane appeared now to be lying on its right-hand side.

Chapter XV

OMAR AND I shared an affinity that I couldn't always accurately define. We also looked remarkably alike. Yet while we spent a lot of time together, we assumed that this happened simply by chance. We were always side by side: during our childhood holidays, our teenage years and then at university, where we studied different subjects. On reaching adulthood, we crossed paths rather bizarrely at various airports around the country, always by coincidence.

Truth be told, I felt no real compassion for the crushing sense of guilt that was gnawing away at Omar, nor for the shame he endured on behalf of his father and his younger brother, since he would accuse them rabidly one day, while passionately defending them the next. I did not therefore have much pity for his supposedly harrowing situation, since it had become a game to him – a kind of masochism that gave his life both meaning and a sense of direction.

And yet Omar appealed to me for a reason I not only refused to admit, but which also embarrassed me so much that I hid it from him for many years. Omar's father, Uncle Kamal, had suffered the ups and downs of the war and had been a victim of history's contradictions, as well as a victim of his own enigmatic nature, of his running with the hare and hunting with the hounds. Omar simply had to come to terms with that!

His younger brother, however, bore full responsibility for

his actions, having joined the OAS out of pure cowardice. He had taken up arms against his own people, targeted members of the Organisation and wrought havoc everywhere he went.

When the war began, Omar's father had been Police Commissioner in Batna, the administrative centre of the Aurès region. At which point he immediately reached out to the Organisation, asking his father, Si Mustafa, a life-long nationalist, to intercede with them on his behalf. Uncle Kamal asked the local Organisation boss what to do. Should he resign or remain in his position? The reply was quick and unequivocal: 'You are to remain in your post, as you will be of greater use to us there, rather than in the bush or anywhere else! Make no mistake, however: *we* are now in charge of Batna's police. You will take your orders from us. No dirty tricks!'

A few days later, Uncle Kamal met a representative from the Organisation and a deal was struck. However, the agreement was purely verbal; there were no minutes of the meeting, no papers were signed. It was entirely unofficial, off the books. The Police Commissioner kept his end of the bargain. He must, however, have been a double agent somewhere along the line, simply to allay the suspicions of the French authorities. Did he take it too far? Did he step up his Frenchness to maintain appearances? Overcompensate by mingling in colonial circles more than ever before, attending their parties and even their church services? Of course! It was all part of his strategy, part of his act.

When Independence was declared, Uncle Kamal was stripped of his rank and sent home. He was gravely disappointed. He closeted himself away. Let himself go. Wound up losing his mind. Took to roaming the dirty streets of the city, mumbling incoherently – carrying on this manner for three years right up to his death in 1965.

As soon as the French left, Salim was abducted and almost certainly had his throat slit and his body buried in a forest on the outskirts of the city. All of which added to Uncle Kamal's grief, pushing him further and further into sweet, serene madness.

Si Mustafa, Omar's grandfather, stoically resigned himself to his son's death and his grandson's disappearance. He was brave in the face of adversity, a staunch nationalist as well as proud. He never spoke about this family tragedy, of the injustice heaped on his eldest son or the savage manner in which his grandson had been murdered. Si Mustafa had been disgusted by Salim's actions and refused to speak to him after he became one of the OAS's highest-ranking officers in Batna.

He stood proud, head up. Just like his Barbary figs. He even began to resemble them. Unruffled. Never mentioning the tragedy that had befallen his family to the day he died, never speaking of the unpardonable shame of being seen as the father *and* grandfather of two traitors, two collaborators, he who had dedicated his entire life and wealth to the cause of Independence!

Whenever I spoke of these matters to Omar, I often compared him (when he had gone into the bush) to his grandfather, who had spent a dozen years in a colonial prison cell, his father, who had lacked the courage to break ranks with the French and publicly join the resistance, and his younger brother, who went ahead and turned his back on the Organisation and repeatedly lashed out at it, all in the name of bedding colonial girls and currying favour with their fathers. Who was so blind and in thrall to his French masters that he thought Algeria would never become independent. Omar, however, repeatedly refused to face the facts, telling me point-blank,

'My father! He had wanted to resign! But the Organisation ordered him to stay put. And in the end he was dumped as a traitor and doomed to madness. As for Salim, there's no proof that he was active in the OAS or for that matter even a sympathiser. Absolutely no proof! Do you have any proof? Name a single instance! Just one…' He had flown into a rage. His eyes were full of tears. I felt sorry for him. I kept my mouth shut. Then I left, knowing there was nothing I could do. Knowing that Omar would always remain convinced of his father's and younger brother's innocence. But that he would forever be riven by doubt!

Colonialism was in effect a chronic disease. Both unrelenting and incurable. Almost fifty years after Algeria won its independence, this chicanery continued to make the world suffer. Like leprosy. Indelible. It would take generation upon generation to soothe Algeria's collective consciousness. For the moment, the country was still in the grip of misery: choleric, and on its toes. After such systemic slaughter: massacres, killing sprees, beheadings, summary executions, trips into the countryside where prisoners were shot, buried and never seen or heard from ever again, napalm being dropped over the whole country, nuclear tests in the Sahara. Devastation!

Perhaps all of these things played a part in my fondness for Omar, helping me to come to terms with his irrational desire to clear his younger brother and father of any wrongdoing. He had become paranoid and I liked his paranoia, which had ensured he remained a confirmed and uncompromising bachelor. Had I sought to emulate him by refusing to marry? By choosing to live alone with only Nana and Mozart to keep me company? By working 12 hour days? By spending all my nights either in solitude, with Omar, or with some mistress or other who was just as neurotic, prone to drunkenness and as obsessed as I was with this unspeakable mess? Yet aside from the family and the colonial disasters whose consequences were still so keenly felt after all this time, there was something else that tied me physically and emotionally to Omar. Our childhood days spent on his grandfather's farms? Our teenage years in those seaside cottages where we had first tasted love and had our first sexual experiences? The superb clothes and shoes he would insist on lending me?

His grandfather's cottages had been built on stilts and had stunning, spacious sun decks that looked out over the open sea, since they were located in spots of a singular, breathtaking beauty with unobstructed views. All the best beaches in the east of the country belonged to us: those in Tighzirt, Les Aiguades, Ziana, Cap Bon, Monkey Mountain, Djidjelli, La Calle, Collo...

Of all those joyful memories, our infatuation with the baking summers, our endless swims and our passionate affairs, there was one adventure I'd had with Omar that I continually turned over in my mind.

We were 16 years old when we first made the acquaintance of twin sisters our age. One of them fell head over heels for Omar. But since the sisters were inseparable, Omar was forced to go out on dates with both of them. This uncomfortable situation became even more untenable when the other twin declared that she couldn't help falling in love with the same boy as her sister. Omar took it to heart, telling me, 'They're crazy!'

'No,' I said, 'they're twins'.

As the days went by, I began to hang out with the trio, Omar insisting that one of them should fall for me. The twins had no objections on the condition that the four of us would all make love together. And that was what happened. Over the course of the following summers, Omar and I made love to the twins indiscriminately. Without knowing which was which. Mounia and Dounia were interchangeable and insatiable. They had lured us into a game that both fired us up and terrified us. We were like putty in their hands, which were experienced beyond their years, but the worst thing was that we could never tell them apart. The two sisters were interchangeable and delighted in our confusion.

We were drunk and in high spirits. We had misgivings and regrets. Our foursomes were incestuous, and Omar and I were greatly embarrassed when we came face to face. We sometimes shyly suggested the rules of the games be changed, but the twins always reacted negatively, violently even. Calling us prudes, cowards and homophobic. At which point we gave ground and resumed our frolicking with renewed vigour...

This incredible adventure lasted right up to Omar's leaving the country to study architecture in Paris. I, on the other hand, was still at secondary school. Our relationship with the twins was over. They disappeared! It was Omar they were really after. I was only second string, second fiddle.

A month later, on 1 November 1954, war broke out.

This adventure with the twins forged a deep-seated complicity between Omar and me. That was the real reason behind my affinity for him.

Ever since September 1957, when Omar went into the bush, we had never once spoken about the twins, although they continued to haunt us. As did their anti-conformism – shocking by the standards of the time – their flawless looks, their unbridled sexuality, their proverbial eccentricity, the mad, extravagant laughter they would break into simultaneously and that

Omar and I were never able to predict. The girls had turned us into their sexual slaves.

During this flight from Algiers to Constantine, I admitted to Omar that I had corresponded for a long while with one of the twins while I was in the bush and he was recuperating in Moscow. Omar burst out laughing at this unexpected confession and at the pathetic embarrassment on my face.

He said, 'Oh, those two! But why the long face? They were in love with both of us, as a package. So what? What really matters is that they were a great fuck!'

Omar's attitude and the manner in which he had spoken intrigued me. It seemed too casual. Out of keeping with his usual character.

We were the ones who had fallen in love. That's why we had never married. I had finally found the key to the mystery of our bachelorhood.

Our affair with twins had merely been a conductor, facilitating our relationship in that chauvinistic environment we lived in. They became our role models. Transgressive. Flamboyant. Carnal. Inflammatory. Lesbians. Incestuous. That was why they had captivated us.

The twins were unique, and as a result irreplaceable.

That was it! Sat on that plane, it took me some time to fully realise the extent to which this episode in our lives had shaped us. Omar and I had hidden our love and respect for the twins because our prudishness as adults had imposed on us a soul-crushing morality, which we despised above all else.

I was relieved. Omar seemed at peace. I had not seen him this calm in a long time. Since our teenage years in fact. I was determined to start from scratch as soon as we got to Constantine.

Had Omar finally exorcised his demons during this flight, throughout which we had kept mulling over our feelings of guilt and shame, as well as the entire history of a country that had been invaded, colonised, partitioned and betrayed over and over again, both by outsiders and its own people?

I couldn't be sure.

The plane made a perfectly smooth landing.

A few passengers applauded this minor feat.

In her suave voice, the air hostess welcomed us to Constantine.

Afterword

FROM 1957 UNTIL 1964, when it was re-launched as *Le Nouvel Observateur*, Marguerite Duras wrote a number of incendiary articles for the *France Observateur*: 'Like you, like anyone,' she recalled in 1980, 'I felt an overwhelming urge to denounce injustice of all sorts, whether its victim was a single person or an entire nation.' Her very first piece was entitled 'The Algerian's Flowers', where she described a 'miserably dressed' twenty-year-old Algerian flower seller:

He walks towards the corner of Jacob and Bonaparte, which is less closely watched than the market, and stops there – anxious, of course. He has reason to be anxious. Not ten minutes have passed – he hasn't had the time to sell a single bouquet – when two gentlemen 'in plain clothes' move towards him. They come from rue Bonaparte. They're hunting. Noses in the wind, sniffing the fine Sunday air for irregularities the way a big dog might sniff for quail, they head straight for their quarry.

'Papers?'

The Algerian has no licence to sell flowers.

So one of the two gentlemen goes over to the pushcart, slides his clenched fist underneath, and – how strong he is! – overturns the cart, flowers and all, with a single blow.

The intersection fills with the flowers of early spring (Algerian spring).

Eisenstein isn't there to record that image of flowers on the ground, stared at by the young Algerian flanked by France's representatives of law and order. Nobody is there. The first passing cars avoid the flowers, instinctively drive around them – nobody can stop them from doing that.

No one is there. But wait, yes, there is someone, a woman, just one woman. 'Bravo!' she shouts. 'If the cops always went after them like that, we'd soon be rid of that scum. Bravo!'

When Duras wrote a similar article a year later – this time on the senseless humiliation (and incarceration) inflicted on a North African bartender for the sole reason that he was accompanying a French waitress home – she ended it with the following postscript: 'The person who telephoned me at midnight the last time I dared to speak of "Algerians" and who threatened to "bust my face if I did it again" is kindly requested to leave his name.' It seems Duras took the advice with a pinch of salt, since she later went on to hide members of the clandestine FLN – the *Front de Libération Nationale*, the spearhead of the Algerian liberation movement – in her flat. Such dedication is hardly surprising considering that, as early as 1955, barely a year after the struggle for independence had begun, Duras, alongside André Breton and François Mauriac, had been one of the chief architects behind a petition against the war in North Africa, which incurred the wrath of Jacques Soustelle, the Governor-General of Algeria – who not only rejected the notion that there was even a war in Algeria, but who further opined that it was only a ruse on the part of a handful of 'agitated' intellectuals.

Clear-eyed and fearless in the way they linked colonialism abroad with mounting racism at home – once even drawing parallels between the conditions of Algerian immigrants in Paris and that of the Jews in the Warsaw ghetto – Duras's articles during those years were alas but a premonition of the horrors to come. On 17 October 1961, a peaceful pro-FLN demonstration was attacked by the Parisian police, resulting in 11,538 arrests, at least 200 deaths and a further several hundred who 'disappeared', their bodies most likely quickly (and quietly) consigned to the Seine. Largely unreported in the national press, the cover-up of this massacre proved so efficient that many of the inhabitants in nearby arrondissements were none the wiser until years after the event.[1] Of course, Duras was only one of the many writers and activists who ran considerable risks in reporting the truth. There was, after all, a violent sense of obstinacy in the air, fuelled by the refusal of successive governments to face the inescapable reality on the ground in Algeria – namely, that while the French had actually won the war from a purely military perspective, it was only a matter of time before they would be forced to concede defeat and cut their losses.[2] Yet despite the growing calls for Algerian self-determination on both sides of the Mediterranean – as well as abroad – politicians of all stripes proudly proclaimed their indifference to the popular will: from François Mitterrand's claim that 'Algeria is France' in 1954, to Charles de Gaulle's 1958 speech in Oran when he shouted 'Vive l'Algérie française!'.

Defying this cross-spectrum consensus, Duras, like the overwhelming majority of the French intellectual establishment, continued in her defiance and later became a signatory of the 'Manifesto of the 121', the now famous open letter published in 1960, which levelled a number of accusations against the French government – and was one of the few instances that saw the Left and Right united under a single cause; proof yet again of France's 'special' relationship with that country, which it had officially annexed in 1848, 18 years after it was conquered and its population subjected to one of the first modern instances of systematic ethnic genocide. Even the easily distracted Napoleon III had a soft spot for Algeria, fancying himself not only the Emperor of the French, but of the Arabs too. Yet if France singled Algeria out for preferential treatment, it did so in a variety of manners: long before Polynesia, Algeria was France's first and favoured testing site for its nuclear programme, whose crowning moment came on 13 February 1960, when a Hiroshima-style bomb was detonated just outside the small oasis of Reggane, deep in the Saharan south – subjecting thousands of civilians to critical levels of radiation. The majority of them are still awaiting compensation, despite the fact that 2012 marks the 50th anniversary of Algerian independence – all of which is unsurprising considering that France only recognised the Algerian conflict as a 'war' as late as 1999.[3]

The events of the Algerian war (1954–1962) have inspired countless histories, novels, memoirs and films, and yet there is no single writer that has so singularly devoted himself to the task of tackling the mind-boggling ramifications of that conflict – in both France and Algeria – as Rashid Boudjedra. Born on 5 September 1941 in Aïn Beïda, a small city to the southeast of Constantine, Boudjedra moved to Tunis at the age of ten, when his father, a wealthy merchant, sent him to attend the elite Collège Sadiki[4] where he received a solid grounding in both Arabic and French. Aged 17, Boudjedra left Tunis and returned to Algeria, where he joined the FLN, which had been fighting against the French since 1954. Wounded after a few months of active service, Boudjedra spent the following couple of years as the FLN's representative in Madrid. Back in Algeria in time for Independence in 1962, Boudjedra began an undergraduate degree in philosophy, which he completed at the Sorbonne in 1965, and subsequently wrote a master's thesis on the works of Louis-Ferdinand Céline. Later that year, Boudjedra published *Pour ne plus rêver* (*To No Longer Dream*), a collection of poetry championed by Jean Sénac[5], one of Algeria's leading poets. By the time Boudjedra returned to Algiers, the country's post-colonial transition was entering a violent, authoritarian phase; the same country that had once welcomed Malcolm X and Che Guevara was now suppressing the trade union movement and routinely 'disappearing' or forcing into exile the *pieds rouges*, who unlike the *pieds noirs* had been pro-independence, definitively brushing aside the promise of the early years, when Ahmed Ben Bella – who passed away this April – would pose for photographs in his blue Mao jacket and declare that Algeria would serve as 'a beacon' to the Third World. Ben Bella was eventually ousted in June 1965 by Houari Boumédienne, his minister of defence,[6] and an atmosphere of political intolerance quickly ensued, making life very difficult for outspoken leftists such as Boudjedra, whose criticisms of the government not only lost him his job, but further earnt him a two-year sentence in prison. Released in 1967, Boudjedra was then exiled to Blida, to the south-west of Algiers. During that time, he taught at the Lycée El Feth, a girls' high school, an experience that allowed him to witness first-hand the challenges, dogmas and taboos faced by young Algerian women, and which later served as the inspiration for his second novel, *L'Insolation* (*Sunstroke*).

While in Blida, Boudjedra began his first novel, *La Répudia-tion* (*The Repudiation*), a thinly veiled autobiographical account of how his mother was cast aside by her husband on a spurious charge of adultery after he decided to take on a younger wife, and who was then kept a virtual prisoner in her own home: 'The cloistering was necessary, inevitable, and would last for the rest of her life.' A violent and erotic journey into the psyche of the narrator, a young Algerian, as he describes these events to his lover, Céline, a Frenchwoman, *The Repudiation* also features 'Si Zoubir', or 'Mr Prick', the domineering father, as well as Zahir, the narrator's older brother, a tormented homosexual who ulti-mately takes his own life at the age of 20 after a failed romance with a Jewish professor. Immediately banned in Algeria due to its sexual content – one of the book's most amusing scenes features a pederastic Qur'anic schoolmaster – and the ferocious way in which it assailed that society's deep-seated prejudices regarding women, Jews and political dissenters, its publication marked a watershed in North Africa letters. Despite forcing the author into exile after a fatwa – the first of many – was pronounced against him, the book was nevertheless the subject of immense acclaim in France, where it was awarded Jean Coc-teau's Prix des Enfants Terribles.

While in exile in Paris, Boudjedra produced a series of long journalistic essays: *La Vie quotidienne en Algérie* (*Daily Life in Algeria*) and *Naissance du cinéma algérien* (*The Birth of Algerian Cinema*) in 1971, and *Journal Palestinien* (*Palestinian Diary*) in 1972 – by which time he had also published his second novel *L'Insolation* and relocated to Rabat in Morocco, where he would remain until 1975. That year, Mohamed Lakhdar-Hamina's *Chronique des années de braise* (*Chronicle of the Years of Fire*), on which Boudjedra had worked as a screenwriter and which narrated the events of the War of Independence through the eyes of a peasant, was awarded the Palme d'Or at the Cannes Film Festival. By the mid 1970s, the political situation in Algeria had turned somewhat more favourable: after the failed collectivisation of agriculture, a new constitution was introduced and the FLN decided to relax their grip on the country's political life, opting for a rapprochement with the Communists, allowing a number of intellectuals some sway over governmental policy – all of which prompted Boudjedra to return. Around this time, he served briefly as an adviser to the Ministry of Culture, contributed to the *Révolution Africaine*, a journal that supported the Third World, and became a founding member of the Algerian League for the Defence of Human Rights.

The late 1970s and early 1980s were a prolific time for Boudjedra, beginning with 1975's *Topographie idéale pour une agression caractérisée* (*Ideal topography for an aggravated assault*): the story of an illiterate immigrant lost in the Paris metro who is murdered by xenophobes as he is unable to read the maps and find his way out; then 1977's *L'Escargot entêté* (*The Stubborn Snail*), a Kafkaesque parody of six days in the life of the head of the 'Department for the Destruction of Rats', who conscientiously carries out his duties despite his love for the animals until he encounters a gargantuan snail.[7] Boudjedra followed this up two years later with 1979's *Les 1001 années de la nostalgie* (*The 1001 Years of Nostalgia*), a sprawling fable that focuses on a Saharan village trying to survive in the face of modernity as it interacts with an American film crew shooting on location; and 1981's *Le Vainqueur de coupe* (*The Cupwinner*): a brilliant recreation of the assassination of Ali Chekkal, a pro-French Algerian politician during a football cup final in 1957.

Le Vainqueur de coupe was the last novel Boudjedra would write in French until the mid-1990s. Beginning with 1982's *Al-Tafakkuk*, the story of two women's struggle to break out of their feudal bonds in the aftermath of independence, Boudjedra abandoned that language in favour of Arabic, while ensuring his books were immediately translated into French. This, as Boudjedra contends, was part of his attempt to modernise the Arabic novel and steer it away from the 19th-century model popularised by writers like Naguib Mahfouz. While Boudjedra initially attempted to translate these books himself, as he did with *Al-Tafakkuk*, which later appeared as *Le Démantèlement* (*The Unravelling*), he found he was not suited to the task, as it proved too great a temptation to revise and rewrite. For his following four novels, Boudjedra therefore collaborated with Father Antoine Moussali (1920–2003) – a Lazarist priest of Lebanese origins who worked for Diocese of Algiers and taught Arabic at the local university. Together, Boudjedra and Moussali co-translated *La Macération* (*The Maceration*) in 1984, *La Pluie* (*The Rain*) and *La Prise de Gibraltar* (*The Taking of Gibraltar*) in 1987, and *Le Désordre des choses* (*The Disorder of Things*) in 1991.

Restlessly outspoken, Boudjedra earned himself a second fatwa in 1986 when he contributed to *L'Islam en Questions*, for which 24 Arab writers were asked whether Islam could prove a workable template for a modern state. Boudjedra's reply was the following:

No, absolutely not. It's impossible; that is not just a personal opinion, it's something objective. We saw that when Nimeiry [Sudanese Head of State] wanted to apply Sharia law: it didn't work. The experiment ended abruptly after some hands and feet were chopped off... There is a reaction even among the mass of Muslims against this sort of thing – stoning women, for example, is hardly carried out, except in Saudi Arabia, and even then extremely rarely... Islam is absolutely incompatible with a modern state... No, I don't see how Islam could be a system of government.

Several of the comments Boudjedra made were later expanded upon in 1992's *FIS de la haine* (*The Sons of Hate*)[8], an explosive indictment of Algeria's increasingly popular FIS – *Front Islamique du Salut* – whom Boudjedra excoriated, comparing them, among other things, to the Nazis:

> Between the fire at the Reichstag in 1933 and the fire in the little apartment in Ouargla in 1989 [when the house of a widowed woman suspected of receiving male guests was set on fire, killing her child and causing third degree burns to her face], there is more than an analogy. There is the whole world of barbarity and insanity.

The book's publication coincided with the beginning of the Algerian Civil War (1992–2002) which was a result of the military's intervention to prevent the FIS from taking power after it gained a majority in Algeria's first democratic elections. *FIS de la haine* marked Boudjedra's return to French and he subsequently published a novel *Timimoun* (1994), a play, *Mines de rien* (*As if Nothing Had Happened*); the non-fiction *Lettres algériennes* (*Letters from Algeria*) in 1995, *La Vie à l'endroit* (*Life Right Side Up*) in 1997, *Fascination* in 2000, *Les Funérailles*, (*The Funerals*) and a book-length essay about the visual arts, *Peindre l'Orient* (*Painting the Orient*) in 2003; *Hôtel Saint Georges* and

Cinq Fragments du désert (*Five Fragments of the Desert*) in 2007
and *Les Figuiers de Barbarie* (*The Barbary Figs*) in 2010.

Described by Boudjedra as 'the novel of my life', *The Barbary
Figs* takes place in a single hour, during which two once-insep-
arable cousins,[9] Rashid and Omar, find themselves on a flight
from Algiers to Constantine. As the plane takes off, Rashid
begins to relive the traumas of Algeria's past, taking the reader
on a macabre ride through a historical hall of horrors, from
1830 to the present day, using his own life and that of his cousin
– the novel is in a sense the biography of both – as a prism,
sliding from one scene to the next, utterly radical in its pursuit
of truth, and, he hopes, closure. The only comparable novel
that springs to mind is Wolfgang Koeppen's masterly *Death
in Rome*, though the historical element in *The Barbary Figs* is
less of a micro-plot than it is a major part of the tapestry. The
narrator aides his quest by recalling old newspaper headlines –
'THERE MUST BE A RUTHLESS CLAMPDOWN, GEN-
TLEMEN! FRANCE REACHES FROM FLANDERS TO
THE CONGO!' – lessons imparted by his teachers – including a story about how Marseille's famous soap was once manu-
factured using human remains looted from Muslim cemeteries
– as well as chilling extracts from letters the French General
Saint-Arnaud (1801–1854) sent home to his family – 'Frankly
speaking, brother, Algeria simply loses its poetry without a
good deal of massacres and smoke-outs.' Rashid thereby ushers
us into a painstakingly researched world, and after a few pages,
we begin to share in Rashid's belief that though some questions
may remain unanswerable, it is nonetheless vital to raise them.
This is Boudjedra's greatest success in *The Barbary Figs*: to make
these questions relevant whether one likes these characters or

not. Omar's crippling doubts as to whether his father really did collaborate with the French during the resistance, an ambiguity that eventually leads to public dishonour, and later insanity and death, becomes pertinent to us; as does what is perhaps the most important of these questions: was Algerian independence simply the precursor to even greater crimes against the Algerian people? Yet above all, *The Barbary Figs* is a eulogy to the lives lost not only in Algeria, but in *all* colonial wars:

War, this carnival to which foolish soldiers traipsed off and always lost, trudging through the muddy Vietnamese marshes, catching all sorts of diseases like foot-and-mouth, yellow fever, dying as they cried out for their mothers, their mouths full of mosquitoes, their flocculent bodies slowly decomposing, rotting, deteriorating in a very short space of time because the tropical climate is quicker than any ambulance, any rescue helicopter, any combat fighter, any chemical or nuclear weapon... Bubbling with heat, its slimy, marshy vapours and that unbelievable sweat trickling from God knows where, as if the body was capable of pumping it up and out again at a frightening pace.

These stupid, perennial losers of the colonial wars, yomping through the icy Algerian winters and the mossy Vietnamese jungle, contracting all types of hepatitis, dying as they cried out for their fathers, their mouth full of ants, their frozen bodies washed away by the mad, raging streams flooding down from the Atlas mountains, bodies later found torn to shreds in oases like Mchounèche, Tolga and Timimoun, where the first heat waves of the Saharan spring stripped them to the bone in the blink of an eye, helped by voracious horned vipers and the countless ants...

Yet the Algeria Rashid and Omar return to after the war is in the full grip of retribution and paranoia. Not long after independence, Rashid is almost torn to shreds by an angry crowd when his blond hair and light skin mark him out as a traitor: a fate he is spared by an old woman's timely intervention, who argues that 'despite' the colour of his skin, or that of his hair, there is 'something Algerian' about him.

Rashid and Omar's anxieties over their identities are exacerbated when their legacy as freedom fighters is fatally compromised by the FLN's – always referred to as the 'Organisation' – brutal repression of the October riots in 1988, when a sharp drop in petroleum prices seriously affected Algeria's economy, to the point that the government found itself unable to pay the country's civil servants and the cost of living rose dramatically, sparking off a series of protests. By virtue of honest, rhythmic prose, we are made to feel Rashid's disappointment and overwhelming sense of impotence as he telephones Omar. We cringe as the cousins commiserate over the country's tragic state of affairs as they witness former brothers-in-arms – now turned party supremos and wealthy autocrats – dispatch young soldiers to spill the blood of their own countrymen:

> I was appalled, stricken with chronic grief and melancholia as I watched Algerian soldiers, of all people, savagely putting down those angry riots during that mild month of October 1988. I ached all over, as if I had been torn apart.

While the events of October 1988 initially led to a new constitution, which was theoretically supposed to dismantle the FLN's supremacy, the long-awaited democratic elections that followed in 1990, whose results the FLN refused to recognise, ironically led to the civil war and the perpetuation of the one-party state.

Keeping hope alive in such dire circumstances becomes an exceptional feat, yet it is one that Rashid is determined to attempt, despite the best efforts of his twin brother, Zygote, who arguably serves as his alter ego: the evil other, small-minded, green-eyed, indifferent to the tragedies taking place everywhere around him. The material representation of hope comes in the form of the Barbary figs, the central metaphor of the novel, and an omnipresent part of the Algerian landscape – the plant is a recurring motif: appearing in a golden effigy around Omar's neck and among the 'the charred remains of Jeeps, disembowelled tanks, the fragments of shrapnel and the mines buried just under the scree that was sullied for miles on end with napalm' as Rashid winds his way through the bush as a rebel, and finally, as an eternal symbol of resistance.

> Those Barbary figs had been a staple part of our summer hol-idays, their different shades – ranging from green to brown and red – with that trademark stiffness that made them seem so much more violent to us, so much more real. [...] To us, the Barbary figs were symbolic guardians that had always kept watch over our country. Despite all the disasters and the trag-edies, despite the genocide!

No single emblem better sums up Boudjedra's desire to reclaim history in the face of defeat, especially considering that *figuiers* was also a racial slur used by the French to refer to the Algerians during the war.

Central to Boudjedra's ambitious project is his willingness to experiment. Just as William Faulkner intended *The Sound and the Fury* to be published in different coloured inks to differentiate his storylines, Boudjedra builds a labyrinth of digressions within digressions, purposefully scrambling our sense of plot in order to make our thought processes, doubts and revelations keep pace with that of the narrator. That Boudjedra achieves this by appropriating Céline's notoriously difficult punctuation makes his an even more remarkable accomplishment. Heavily influenced by Claude Simon and the *nouveau roman*, Boudjedra writes in a style that may be termed 'verbal excess', constantly reiterating key themes and obsessions, endowing his prose with a hallucinatory quality, thereby indirectly achieving a grotesque sort of realism, where every detail acquires a visceral vividness. Boudjedra adds to this disorientation by inducing a sense of déjà vu by sometimes transposing entire pages from an old novel into a new one, creating an intertextual continuity throughout his oeuvre.[10]

To my knowledge, Boudjedra is the only living writer to have successfully switched from French to Arabic and back again. In interviews, Boudjedra has often attributed his decision to switch languages mid-career to his wanting to reconnect with Algeria's identity and bring himself closer to his mother tongue, recalling the case of his mother, who only spoke the Algerian dialect of that language. Comfortable in two languages – like Isaac Singer, Joseph Conrad, Vladimir Nabokov, Samuel Beckett, Czeslaw Milosz, Julien Green, Milan Kundera and André Brink before him – Boudjedra's example however corresponds more closely to that of Ngugi wa Thiong'o, since both were primarily driven by a political dissatisfaction with their respective colonial languages.

Regardless of the language in which they were written, or

the themes they tackle, once Boudjedra's novels are pieced together, like the tiles of a mosaic or the pieces of jigsaw puzzle, the vivid, layered complexity of the Algeria they depict falls nowhere short of William Faulkner's Yoknapatawpha County or Émile Zola's *Les Rougon-Macquart*. They are a crescendo of clarity, sifting through the bloody rubble of history and broken lives, affording a rare glimpse into that shameful recess of the collective Franco-Algerian conscience. Anyone interested by Alexis de Tocqueville's contention that colonisation made Muslim society more barbaric than it was before the French arrived will find Boudjedra's work essential reading.

From *La Pluie* (1987) where Boudjedra recounts the bigotry and sexism faced by the female head of a health clinic, to *La Vie à l'endroit* (1997), the tale of a man pursued by assassins because of his political beliefs, all the way to *Les Funérailles*, (2003), a disturbing look at religious fanaticism during the civil war through the eyes of Sarah, a detective in the anti-terrorist brigade, Boudjedra's novels represent one of the most outstanding testaments to the lives trapped in the Serbonian bog of history. They are bleak, disheartening and yet strangely life-affirming books, simply because Boudjedra appears to have hung on to his firm belief in the potential of literature to contribute to the formation of a responsible and engaged citizenry, whose knowledge of history and its consequences can ultimately be a force for good. In *Letters from Algeria* (1995), Boudjedra describes his view on the relationship between history and literature:

All great literature has incorporated history as a fundamental element of the interrogation between the real and the human, operating in a more subjective mode than one would think in so far as it is the one fruitful and interesting mode of inquiry, becoming far more than just a reading of the past that is immediate, official, fossilized, academic, mechanistic and opportunistic, always co-opted, distorted and travestied for the sake of the cause.

Boudjedra occupies a position at the very forefront of modern North African literature, yet this recognition has thus far been restricted to academic circles. The reasons for this are manifold: chief among them that the majority of Arabic literature selected for translation – especially in English – conform to the old stereotypes: Allah, the subjugation of women, and sexually frustrated would-be terrorists. The five years since the International Prize for Arabic Fiction (IPAF) was set up have seen three of those awards bestowed on what I believe are timid historical novels, in what seems to be a concerted effort to favour mediocre works of fantasy over a more serious, and potentially compromising sort of literature. Yet if apathy is to be our fate, and as Sartre once wrote, we are to enter century after century groping blindly along, then how to reconcile our consciences? Boudjedra's may be an uncomfortable voice, but it is inescapable, and haunting.

As Doris Lessing remarked in her Massey Lectures, 'To remember history is not for the sake of keeping alive the memories of old tyrannies, but to recognise present tyranny, for these patterns are in us still.' To read Rashid Boudjedra's novels is to understand – and feel – how sane men and women can be led down the road of murder and madness in times of public lunacy. There is no single truth to be found in his books, no one-sided aim other than the faithful record of the atrocities committed during those terrible years, atrocities that went well beyond those usually licensed by war. Reading his novels is a rewarding and gut-twistingly *human* experience. Why? Because we should all be very frightened about what happened, and continues to happen, in Algeria.

André Naffis-Sahely
London, July 2012

Notes

1 The atrocity was first commemorated publicly in 1990.

2 Though Algeria had become a veritable fortress of horror in the years 1954–1962 – which saw the sealing of the borders with Tunisia and Morocco, the carpet bombing of rural communities and urban centres (the most famous being the so-called Battle of Algiers that took place between September 1956 and September 1957) – the increasing acts of sabotage, international pressure and mounting expenditures made France's dream of keeping Algeria untenable.

3 In 2006, François Hollande went on record as saying that 'we still owe an apology to the Algerian people.'

4 Situated in an old Janissary barracks in the heart of the kasbah, the Collège Sadiki had been established in 1875 by Khair al-Din Pasha, the Grand Vizier of Tunisia, in order to provide the next generation of Ottoman officials with a modern education. Six years later, the French invaded Tunisia, bringing three centuries of rule by the Sublime Porte to an end. Tunisia would remain in French hands until 1956.

5 Sénac, an old friend of Camus' until their public split over the issue of Algerian Independence, was one of the few *pieds noirs* to remain in the country. His murder in 1973 remains unsolved.

6 Ben Bella was placed under house arrest until 1980, when he was allowed to go into exile in Switzerland.

7 One of Boudjedra's most successful works – the Russian translation sold over a million copies in the Soviet Union.

8 The title in French is a pun: 'FIS' are the initials of the *Front Islamique du Salut* (Islamic Salvation Front), the leading Islamist parties, while 'fils' is French for 'son(s)'.

9 As with all of his novels, *The Barbary Figs* is partly autobiographical. The relationship between Rashid and Omar was apparently based on a similar experience Boudjedra shared with one of his cousins.

10 Some of the passages in *The Barbary Figs* – concerning Rashid's brother Zahir – are taken wholesale from *La Répudiation*, his début.

Glossary

Abd el-Kader (1808–1883). Algerian theologian, philosopher and a leader of the resistance, often seen as a national hero. Abd el-Kader's decade-long guerrilla warfare was initially successful, but due to the unravelling of the alliance of various tribes he had cobbled together and the vast superiority of the French forces, he was forced to surrender in 1847 and was sent into exile. In 1860, during the first Lebanese civil war, Abd el-Kader sheltered 3,000 Christians after the outbreak of communal violence. He died in Damascus.

Abderrahmane, Taleb (1930–1958). A chemistry student who joined the FLN in 1955. He was known as the 'chemist' of the Battle of Algiers due to his alleged bomb-making skills. He was executed in Barbarossa prison on 24 April 1958.

Amirouche, Aït Hamouda (1926–1959). Algerian military leader during the war. A victim of the '*Bleuite*', Amirouche grew convinced he was surrounded by spies, and personally ordered the execution of thousands, based on the false accusations put to him by the real traitors in his entourage. Amirouche was eventually assassinated by the French in 1959.

Amrani, Djamal (1935–2005). Algerian poet who wrote in French. A student activist, Amrani was arrested in 1957 and tortured. Released a year later, he was exiled to France.

Annaba City in Eastern Algeria; formerly Hippo Regius, a major city of Roman Africa, the city was known as Bône during the French colonial period, when it had a sizeable *pied noir* community.

Audin, Maurice (1932–1957). A French mathematics assistant at the University of Algiers, as well as a member of the Algerian Communist Party. His 'disappearance' during the Battle of Algiers remains a mystery despite repeated efforts over the years by his wife and daughters to convince the French authorities to re-open his case. Henri Alleg describes being arrested alongside Audin – who was being tortured when Alleg saw him – in his famous work *La Question* (1958).

Aussaresses, Paul (1918–). Career French soldier who served in the Second World War, Indochina and Algeria. Aussaresses played a controversial role that led to the massacre of Philippeville in August 1955 and was later one the leading French officers during the Battle of Algiers. Suspected of orchestrating Larbi Ben Mhidi's apparent suicide, he confessed to this crime in 2000. After Algeria, Aussaresses trained American troops in counter-insurgency tactics that were later employed in Vietnam. He carried out this work for numerous Latin American dictatorships in the 1970s and 1980s.

Bashagha Of Ottoman origin, from 'Pasha' meaning 'governing noble', or 'high dignitary'.

Belkacem, Krim (1922–1970). One of the founders of the FLN and lead negotiator during the Évian agreements of March 1962 that led to Algerian Independence. Following 1965, Belkacem was ostracised by authoritarian elements in the party, and went into opposition, but was found murdered in a hotel room in Frankfurt in 1970.

Ben Bouali, Hassiba (1938–1957). FLN militant killed during the Battle of Algiers, when her hideout in the Casbah was bombed.

Ben Mhidi, Larbi (1923–1957). Founder and prominent leader of the FLN. Captured in February 1957, he was transferred to Aussaresses's custody, where he was tortured and eventually executed. His body was later taken to a farm where he was hanged in order to make it seem as if he'd taken his own life.

Ben Sadok, Mohammed. Ali Chekkal's assassin. Also the subject of Boudjedra's sixth novel, *Le Vainqueur de coupe* (1981), which recounts the events at the Stade de Colombes from a variety of angles.

Bergson, Henri-Louis (1859–1941). Influential French philosopher who valued intuition above rationalism and was awarded the Nobel Prize in Literature in 1927. Boudjedra makes a veiled reference to his essay *Le rire – Essai sur la signification du comique*, (1900). When Rashid says 'What distinguishes man isn't his capacity to laugh', he is inverting a famous phrase from Rabelais' *Gargantua and Pantagruel*, 'le rire est le propre de l'homme' or 'what distinguishes man is his capacity to laugh'. Bergson contended that laughter and cruelty were closely related; that we laugh at those who fail to adapt to the demands of society.

Bey Vassal sovereign of the Ottoman sultan, governor. Of Turkish origin, and also used in Persia.

Bey, Ahmed (1786–1851). Last Ottoman *Bey* of Constantine who began his rule only four years before the French invasion. He waged an ultimately unsuccessful resistance between 1837 and 1848, when he was finally deposed by the French and Constantine was annexed to Algiers.

Bigeard, Marcel (1916–2010). Alongside Jacques Massu and Paul Aussaresses, Bigeard was one of the key officers spearheading the French effort to crush the FLN's organisation during the Battle of Algiers. After retiring from the military, Bigeard sat as a deputy in the National Assembly.

Biskra Oasis town on the northern edge of the Sahara.

Bleuite Or 'conspiracy of the blues', is a term assigned to a strategy of manipulation designed by the French secret services during the war. It consisted in furnishing the higher echelons of the resistance with falsified lists of supposed traitors, informers and collaborators. The desired result – often very brutally achieved – was to instill an atmosphere of disinformation and paranoia, prompting top commanders to purge some of their best cadres. It led to the ALN (the armed wing of the FLN) losing some of its finest commanders and leaders. Colonel Amirouche is perhaps one of the most infamous targets of this conspiracy.

Bône Former name of Annaba (the ancient Hippo), a city in north-eastern Algeria.

Boupacha, Djamila (1938–). FLN militant who was arrested alongside her family and then raped while in custody. Simone de Beauvoir famously wrote an article in her defence that was published in *Le Monde*, unleashing a storm of media attention. When her case was brought to trial, Boupacha was initially sentenced to death. She was later amnestied in 1962.

Bourmont, Louis (1773–1846). French general and Marshal of France who commanded the invasion of Algeria in 1830. After the July Revolution overthrew Charles X, Bourmont refused to swear allegiance to Louis Philippe, the new king, and was therefore dismissed.

Bournous Long, hooded cloak made of rough wool, worn throughout North Africa.

Boussouf, Abdelhafid (1926–1980). Algerian nationalist and a leader of the FLN, later head of military intelligence. After Independence, he abandoned politics in favour of various business activities.

Bugeaud, Thomas (1784–1849). Beginning in 1836, Bugeaud won a string of victories against the Algerians and was made Governor-General of Algeria in 1841, serving until 1847. He died two years later in Paris.

Caïd The equivalent of a European duke or count, denoting either an administrative, judicial or financial office. Also used to describe the head of a tribe. Such titles, as in Europe, could be bought and sold.

Cavaignac, Louis-Eugène (1802–1857). French general who spent the majority of his career in Algeria (1832–1848), where he quickly rose through the ranks. Known for his efficiency and brutality, Cavaignac was elected to the National Assembly in the aftermath of the 1848 revolution. When the uprisings began in the French capital he was made de facto head of state and dictator, charged with the task of suppressing the insurrection later known as the June Days Uprising. Cavaignac was subsequently a candidate in the presidential elections, which his opponent, Louis-Napoléon Bonaparte – later Napoleon III – won in a landslide. Briefly in opposition, Cavaignac retired from public life after Louis-Napoléon's coup d'état on 2 December 1851 and the subsequent proclamation of the Second French Empire.

Chekkal, Ali (?–1957). Pro-French Algerian politician. Elected to the Algerian Assembly, Chekkal later became its vice-president. Assassinated by the FLN on 26 May 1957 at the Stade de Colombes in Paris.

Chamber of Peers (or 'Chambre des pairs'). French upper house of Parliament that existed between 1814 and 1848, modelled on the British House of Lords. Members were appointed by the king. Victor Hugo was elected to a peerage in 1845.

Clauzel, Bertrand (1772–1842). French general who replaced Bourmont. Marshal of France from 1831, Clauzel won several victories in the early to mid 1830s before being defeated in Constantine in 1836. Dismissed, Clauzel then retired.

Cherchell Seaside town 55 miles west of Algiers.

Djellabah A traditional Moroccan robe worn by men and women alike. It is loose-fitting, long-sleeved, features a hood and is usually maroon or grey.

Drif, Zohra (1934–). FLN militant behind the 1956 Milk Bar Café bombing. Captured in 1957, she was sent to Barbarossa prison and sentenced to 20 years of hard labour, but was released in 1962, when De Gaulle amnestied a number of political prisoners.

DST Acronym for '*Direction de la Surveillance du Territoire*' or 'Directorate of Territorial Surveillance', a French domestic intelligence agency. Its operatives were heavily involved in the Algerian war.

Emir Prince, chief.

Fellagha Literally 'outlaw'. An armed militant or guerrilla belonging to the anti-colonial movements in French North Africa.

FLN Acronym for the '*Front de Libération Nationale*' or 'National Liberation Front'. Originally socialist and anti-colonial in outlook, the FLN was established in November 1954 as a merger of other, smaller groups, to obtain independence for Algeria. Following Independence in 1962, the FLN outlawed all political parties and set up a one-party state. It has been in power ever since. Abdelaziz Bouteflika, the President of Algeria since 1999, is a member of the FLN and was re-elected in 2009 with 90.24% of the vote amidst widespread accusations of fraud.

Gaouri An Algerian of French or European origin. From the Turkish for infidel.

Ghar Cave.

Halva Popular dessert made from tahini (sesame paste) or various other nut-based butters.

Harki(s) Muslim Algerians who served as auxiliaries in the French army.

Jijel Town 90 miles west of Constantine.

Kabyles (from the Arabic for 'tribe'). A community of Berbers whose heartland lies 100 miles east of Algiers. As opposed to Arab Algerians, the Kabyles are largely secular. They represent roughly a quarter of Algeria's total population.

Lalla Fadhma N'Soumer (1830–1863). One of the figureheads of the Kabyle resistance movement during the early years of the French colonial conquest of Algeria. *Lalla* is the female equivalent of *Si* (or *Sidi*). Once Algiers and Constantine had been conquered, Kabylia remained the only region still independent of the French. After leading a long struggle, and a French offensive that saw Kabylia overwhelmed by sheer force of numbers, N'Soumer was taken and placed under house arrest, where she subsequently died. She occupies the same place as Joan of Arc or Boadicea in the Algerian popular consciousness.

Madrasah Qur'anic school.

Marabout A saintly Muslim teacher or holy man, sometimes a hermit and usually distinguished by his asceticism. Marabouts are widely consulted for advice on many material and practical problems. Marabouts can be found in countries all over Northern and Western Africa. Boudjedra, like many other writers from the region, criticises the hold they have over people, especially the uneducated.

Marquet, Albert (1875–1947). French Fauvist painter renowned for his waterfront pictures of Algiers.

Mawlid Festivities marking the birth of the Prophet Mohammed.

Meyssonnier, Fernand (1931–2008). The last executioner in French Algeria from 1958 to 1961. Meyssonnier inherited the job from his father, Maurice, who served in that capacity from 1947 to 1958 when he retired. The epithet 'Mr Algiers' stems from 1870, when the French Third Republic assigned Antoine Rasseneux the title of '*Éxécuteur des Arrêts Criminels en Algérie*', tasking him with all executions in that country. Regulations have since stipulated that the men who occupy this role should be known as 'Mr Algiers'.

Mimoun, Alain (1921–). Algerian athlete and Olympic marathon champion at the 1956 Melbourne Games.

Nabab An Ottoman-era honorific, from the Arabic for governor. A high-ranking official or wealthy landowner.

OAS Acronym for '*Organisation de l'armée secrète*' or 'Secret Army Organisation'. A paramilitary group opposed to Algerian Independence that employed terrorist tactics both in mainland France and in Algeria in order to further its aims. It counted several senior French politicians and military officers among its members. It was responsible for the attempted assassination of President Charles de Gaulle in 1962.

Peschard, Raymonde (1927–1957). *Pied noir* who collaborated with Fernand Yveton. Captured while on the run, the unarmed Peschard was executed on the spot.

Pétainistes Literally followers (or admirers) of Philippe Pétain (1856–1951), also commonly referred to as Maréchal Pétain. An outstanding commander during the First World War, Pétain was later installed as the Chief of State of Vichy France, in which capacity he served from 1940 to 1944. Later tried and convicted of treason, collaborating with the Nazis and various other crimes, his death sentence was commuted to life imprisonment by Charles de Gaulle, a former protégé. 'Pétainistes' is also derogatory term applied to reactionaries.

Pieds noirs While the exact origins of this term (literally 'Black Feet') are the subject of debate, it is now used to describe Algerians of European origin – usually French, Italian and Spanish – who lived in that country from 1830 until 1962. Before Algerian Independence, this cosmopolitan community accounted for just over 10 per cent of the population. Though many *pieds noirs* fought alongside the FLN, the majority – some two million – subsequently fled to France after Independence. Several prominent intellectuals, such as Albert Camus, Louis Althusser and Jacques Derrida hail from this community.

Ramdane, Abbane (1920–1957). Algerian revolutionary, murdered by the FLN due to allegations that he was creating a cult of personality around himself.

Red Hand (or '*Main Rouge*'). The name of a clandestine armed cell set up by the DST in order to assassinate prominent nationalists and intellectuals, as well as political and social activists across North Africa during the 1950s and 1960s.

Saint-Arnaud, Armand (1801–1854). Initially a captain in the Foreign Legion, Saint-Arnaud achieved renown after successfully repressing the rebellion in Kabylia. Later appointed Marshal of France by Napoleon III, he died shortly afterwards while in command of French troops in the Crimean War.

Sarouals Low-crotched, baggy trousers traditionally worn in North Africa.

Sétif University town in north-eastern Algeria, 190 miles east of Algiers in the province of Constantine. Situated a thousand metres above sea level, it is one of the coldest regions of Algeria. It is also the site of the infamous massacres of 1945, which began on May 8 of that year, when a demonstration organised by Algerian nationalists turned violent after a young standard-bearer – waving the Algerian flag – was shot dead by a French official. The army was called in and though the number of casualties is a source of contention, estimates vary between thousands and tens of thousands. The Algerian government's official report put the figure at 45,000.

Shatwa Conical headdress worn by Muslim and Jewish women in Algeria; often adorned with long horizontal rows of silver Ottoman coins.

Sheikh Raymond, Raymond Leyris (1912–1961); a virtuoso *oud* player and singer who belonged to the Algerian Jewish community. Admired by Jews and Muslims alike and given the title of Sheikh, he was assassinated by the FLN in 1961.

Smala An Arab leader's attendants and family, or simply a large family.

Souk(s) Market(s).

Souk Ahras A town in eastern Algeria not far from the border with Tunisia.

Stade de Colombes Olympic stadium in Colombes, near Paris.

Steiner, Annie (1928–). *Pied noir* who was a social worker in Algiers and FLN militant. Sentenced to five years in 1957, she was released in 1961.

Surah Subdivision of the Qur'an, which contains 114 surahs.

Ténès Seaside resort 120 miles west of Algiers.

Tlemcen A town in north-western Algeria.

Valée, Sylvain (1773–1846) Artillery commander in the campaign to take the city of Constantine in 1836. Upon success he was made Governor-General, a post he retained until 1840.

Yveton, Fernand (1926–1957). *Pied noir* of mixed Spanish and French descent, and a member of the Algerian Communist Party. He was guillotined in Barbarossa Prison on 11 February 1957.